NOTHING SACRED

First published 2015 by Australian Scholarly Publishing Pty Ltd
7 Lt Lothian St North, North Melbourne, Victoria 3051
tel 61+3+93296963 / fax 61+3+93295452
aspic@ozemail.com.au / www.scholarly.info

ISBN: 978-1-925333-22-0

Cover design & typesetting by Luke Benge

CONTENTS

DRAMATIS PERSONAE

Clodia	Claudia Metelli, one of three daughters of the Roman patrician, Appius Claudius Pulcher. She changed her name to Clodia.
Clodius	Claudius Pulcher one of Clodia's brothers. He changed his patrician name to Publius Clodius Pulcher.
Metellus	Quintus Caecilius Metellus Celer, husband to Clodia.
Fulvia	Wife of Publius Clodius Pulcher.
Cloelius	Henchman of Clodius.
Cicero	M. Tullius Cicero, Orator and Statesman.
Atticus	Titus Pomponius Atticus, friend of Cicero.
Tiro	Marcus Tullius Tiro, slave then freedman of Cicero.
Caelius	Marcus Caelius Rufus, student of Cicero.

Terentia	First wife of Cicero.
Caesar	Gaius Julius Caesar, General, Politician, formed the First Triumvirate with Pompey and Crassus.
Calpurnia	Third wife of Caesar.
Mark Antony	Marcus Antonius. Associate of Clodius, supporter and General of Caesar during the conquest of Gaul and the Civil War.
Pompey	Gnaeus Pompeius Magnus, also called 'Pompey the Great', joined Caesar and Crassus in the First Triumvirate.
Cornelia	Cornelia Metella, widow of Crassus; fifth wife of Pompey.
Milo	Titus Annius Milo, political agitator, supporter of Pompey, prosecuted for the murder of Clodius.
Crassus	Marcus Licinius Crassus, General and Politician; patron of Caesar. Joined the First Triumvirate alliance with Pompey and Caesar.
Catullus	Gaius Valerius Catullus, poet.
Manius Graechus	'The Greek', a confidant of Catullus.

PROLOGUE

AWAKENING

Through labyrinthine streets,
    our lame procession hobbles
        to mother's tomb on the *Via Appia;*
            litter lurching,
our slaves skidding on the dung-smeared cobbles:

So many dead, so many tombs; they nearly reach the city walls.

Father's hired mourners to wail: won't allow
his children to beat themselves with grief

But when the stranger drops to her knees,
        and ululates in hoots and howls;

When she tugs her hair
        and complicated webs tangle her hands;

When she pounds her forehead on the stones,
            her battered bones offer
                no catharsis,
                    bring no relief.

Clodius reads mother's eulogy
Exemplary matrona
modest faithful chaste;
unsoiled by the common crowd

This inscription   on a nearby tomb:
Passer-by, I met my end: Enjoy your life: Know: you too, must die

To be   of the Claudii Pulchri?

A legacy of bones and ash.

BOUNDARIES

'Clodius, are you awake?'

I clamber beside him on the *cubile*
Before the morning hearth fires are lit

His rhythmic snores make it
easier to tell him where I've been:

'I went to check the seams on mother's tomb …
But ended up at the towering Esquiline.'

I recount the scene at the easternmost city gate:
The sprawling crossroad with roaring bonfires
'round which huddles of shapes stood.
How, instinctively, I pulled back into my hood,
Were they street hawkers or common thugs?
Or the plebs sordida, the great unwashed?
That I passed the putrid *puticuli,*
the huge open pits into which the dead
are
thrown;
Giddy: *I'd held my breath too long.*
How my nostrils flared, forced to inhale
the pestilential air.

'I'll take you next time!'

I jump at Clodius' voice,
rising unexpectedly
like a spectre of the dead,
'So you don't get lost …

But you must stay away from the Esquiline …
That place is cursed!'

I leap up from the *cubile,*

'I don't
    need
        protection!'

Clodius peers askance at me, through one sleepy eye,

'We
  had
    to be born with *genius*,'
    he mutters under his breath.

Let him feign outrage:

The 'we'
    confirms
        my cred;

Juno's guardian spirit is all
                girls
                    usually
                        get.

COMPULSION

'It's too dangerous to take you!'

Clodius hangs his hooded *pallium*
on the wooden rod in the *vestibulum*

So I slip out past the slaves, alone

Past the stone decrees that warn
Keep rubbish beyond the city walls

The decrees are utterly futile: Each dead thing
lies where it is thrown, or where it falls;
Sooner or later, hooves or wheels compel it all
into the drains

Past the *popinae*, the smoky huts,
mercenary to bowel and gut

Past the *exoleti* who whistle men from doorways
'Hey! Bargain for you, baby!'

Past the *meretrices*
and their miserly pimps
who sprawl
on the Temple of Isis' marble steps

Past the Temple
and its swirl of perfume and incense
the solemn chant of initiates praying to the goddess

Past the traders mingling near the eastern wall —
marble obelisks and black granite sphinxes for sale —
galabeyas full

Past the *Vicus Tuscus* where rent boys cost less
than a passable cup of wine.

Past the Forum's south side:
Past the loan sharks who take every opportunity
To swindle you with impunity

At last, from the Servian Wall
it's a short walk along Via Appia
to where mother's tomb lies, undisturbed,
in the redolent shade of conifers

In cool stone; a quiet place

Where everything and nothing
is.

THE LAST NIGHTLY EXCURSION

I'm returning from mother's tomb along the *Sacra Via.*

Suddenly the streets are engorged by peat-bog haze;
Fire's raging through the *insulae,*
the rootless apartment blocks:
six storeys of tinder, thin-walled and rickety;
Yet again an open-hearth flame's run up a wooden beam.

Here's Crassus and his troupe with their water cart:
Bells each side clanging; water sloshing out
as it judders over uneven stones.

No sooner they reach the blaze, I watch them tool down.

I recognise the owner's corpulent sway —
it's the Syrian sausage vendor whose stalls line the *vicos* —

'*Denarii,*' Crassus demands, 'Up front!'

There's a startled snort from the Syrian
who thrusts his meaty neck forward
and whose monstrous hands in huge
billowing

motions
implore

an unimpressed Crassus, leaning heavily on his pick.

'Not even a *sestertius* eh?'

Crassus casts a dubious look,
gives his crotch a hoik.
'In that case,

this service's not available for hire ...

Men, we might as well warm ourselves …

… Since the place is on fire!'

As a tumult of smoke hurls through the air

Crassus makes his only offer —

He's prepared to buy the property

'for a modest sum.'

It's an unbelievable one —

they'll last you …
for a while …'

I pass Clodius his final kit. He swings it over his shoulder
where it hangs with the others like disembowelled intestines

His usual wink   then suddenly he's gone

The shadows have crossed the room
when finally I look down to see
my hands chalky with dust.

66BCE

CATCHING THE AMULET

Finding the tarantula behind the *amphora*
is only half the chase.
Even my slave, Alba, who knows her *culina,*
must set a frenzied pace.
She lurches into a hiss of dialect
to steady her shaking hands.
'Ooo, I'll get you, you brute!'

A flick of her wrist: a scoop of spelt flour
stuns it momentarily:
I anticipate it, yet still
involuntarily flinch when the mound jerks into motion:
Its jaunty shuffle across the stone floor
sprouting dark hairs in twitchy protest.

Undaunted, Alba wields the cleaver:
One swift strike severs
the tarantula's broad *caput*
and two pairs of straggly legs.

In the dumplings of flour and arachnid spill
We locate the worms and harvest them, still twitching.
Alba binds them with the gut skin of a stag, then chuckles
at my grimace as the soft bag nestles my abdomen

'Give it a name, Mistress Clodia, you must activate the spell.'
'Alright, Caesar.'
Alba grins. The *cognomen* means 'hairy'.
Sotto voce she confides, 'I've heard He's an *admissarius*,
a stallion: there's no-one escapes his crotch.'

She nods knowingly

'But that calls for more than a charm!'

With a piercing stare,
                she declares with such enthusiasm
                                she inadvertently spits,

'The Egyptian method!

Those crocodile dung diaphragms,

The *matronas* swear by them.'

DOCTRINA

I'm early enough to see Cicero's *litter*
set down near the *Curia*;
Truly 'the Senator's choice' of meeting place:
how very Cicero —
Although it must be said,
He's pernickety as an old matrona,
And his neck-cricking makes me wince …

I'll suggest we stroll from the *Curia*
Along the cool colonnades
Through the heart of the city, the *Forum*;
Past the mingling citizens;
The centre of attention,
Cicero and his protégé—
Like an arse to underwear —
Kólos kai vráki .

Here he comes, on his toes, with his pigeon-like strut
His left arm — at angles to his protruding gut —
holds his toga's manifold slack

Of late, it must be said, he's been successful.
His oratory's witty and clever.
If I can pull this off: Entry to the Senate!

But now, his solemn greeting, so cursory,
Those formidable pleats at the corner of his mouth;
That involuntary facial twitch …

His hand runs a laboured path across his gut;
His cough, clearly intended to disguise
the vociferous rumblings within earshot;

'Lob-ster … Cae-lius,' he grimaces, 'in late spring?

Any won-der
I've got bad *humours*?'

THE BEAST WITHIN

At the *Circus Maximus*
It's all about *nisi videre et videri*
seeing, and being seen

With a slight rocking action, into the arena
strides a tall beast with a long neck,
patchwork skin
the height of four men

The gasp from the crowd rises as high.

Calpurnia, next to me, cranes to see.
'Clodia!'
she exclaims, squeezing my forearm,
'It can't be!
Inside it, there's another beast!'

And sure enough, Fulvia and Livia,
the finger-pointing matronas either side, agree,
'There!'

A thin grey eel curls upward out of its mouth
and suddenly I can't hear for squeals!

FIRST CATILINARIAN ORATION

'A con-spiracy foments —
tap
tap
tap
like seepage —

Then before us it rises like a dark stain on the hewn stones,
Like the slime on the splashed edge of the fountain.'

I raise the packet of letters:
'Today, as surely as we hold this emergency assembly
In the Temple of Jupiter Stator, Senators;
As surely as it is the eighth day of November;
As surely as my name is Marcus Tullius Cicero;

The Senate will hear plans for a wholesale massacre …

And Senators,'

I allow the letters to flap their weighty significance,

'You will learn why the traitor,
Cat-i-line …
should go into voluntary ex-ile:

For conspi-ring to revolt.'

This unleashes a trummel of muttering
I must snatch into a fistful of silence…

Teasingly I pull undone the string
That binds the *papyrum* wad

'So Senators, let us extract the facts …'

APIARIUM

Cicero's asked the Senate to recess:

I'm hovering near a green basalt bust
when he beckons me to his *curule* chair

He grasps my elbow like a blind man, and implores me,
'Imagine for a moment you are my eyes, Cae-lius,
Tell me what you see.'

'The senators … stroking their beards anxiously …

'And?'

'Hunched over the bench,
Cataline's vulturine frame   seething with wrath…'

'It's invig-orating, don't you think Cae-lius' —
Cicero's face lights up with a simpering smile —
'The vi-bration in the hive?

What about Crassus?'

'He sits alone, nursing his hands …'

'Hmm,' Cicero utters snidely, 'consider this Cae-lius …
Those hands … just last night …'

He flaps the letters in front of me

'Off-loaded this wad into mine …
as if it were an ember,
Not needing money, accept-ing no payment …

How for-tu-it-ous a package, Cae-lius,
To have landed … in his lap:
Given to his doorkeeper by an un-known man …

What do you make of it?'

Then before I have a chance
to answer, he declares,

'I'll tell you what …
More con-spir-ators are afoot,

And what's more, Cae-lius:
Rome: for-tunate in my Consul!'

FOR THE RECORD: LETTER TO TIRO

I wish you weren't so far away. I wish you could have been
Here
Today
To have seen the crowds gather; end of sitting …
Lentulus and his co-conspirators
executed in the *Tulliano* — although Catiline
fled; outside the Senate: applause: '*Pater Patriae!*'
'Cicero! Protector of the Republic!' they chanted. A blaze of torches
illumined the way my supporters led, from the Forum
up to my house on the Palatine

Yet, a short glory's to be mine, apparently there's dissent:
The *populares* have taken up Caesar's eloquent
protest speech for their own ends and of course
there is no precedent

What did they expect?
To have all the conspirators together
in one cell? One cell, Tiro;
For still there is no prison at Rome:

I *simply* did what *anyone* would do:
I made room

65BCE

SALUTARY LESSON

'Cae-lius!'

Before I can even turn,
Cicero's wormy tone
insinuates its way along my spine

'… first you burn your fingers in the Catilinarian affair …
then next I hear, you've slipped away …
To Af-ri-ca …'

Eye to eye, and not;
weasel yellow teeth
in the flash of his smile.

'That Cataline … how eas-ily he makes … friends ...'

words
shaken
from outstretched wings

'As easy as feeding a-corns to swine …'

He's no friend of mine, I counter,

Father sent me to the plantation …

… I needed a year
… to clear my head.

Cicero's lips suddenly generous,

'Your father's a wise man Cae-lius:

Pru-dent not to ru-in a fine career …

I hear
he's got
ex-ten-sive
business holdings

Staffed with protective sub-or-dinates …'

He leans forward, a sardonic glint in his eyes,
squinting
down
his
nose
as if the secret lies
sub rosa

'One's head has its … benefits, Cae-lius.

But One must first learn
How to keep One's head.'

I excuse myself hurriedly

In case he expects
We'll scratch this lesson in wax.

63BCE

CLODIUS RETURNS

'I see what's kept you preoccupied!'

It's been seven years.
Now my brother rushes in
with the urgency of rebellion, winds and tides.

His mere presence stirs up the birds;
They teem shrill, sweeping parabolas under the hemp net.

Clodius grins when he sees the stage
'A *scaena*?'

For poems and plays …
I open my arms wide, as if to recite a line of verse

… a monthly *symposium*

'That's genius!' Clodius suddenly smirks,
'By invitation only …
I bet
Cicero's irked …

And what's this?'

He walks toward the saltwater pond,

'*Pisces*?'

Clodius swirls a fleshy hand across the water's rim

swaying the fronds of the aquatic plants
until the mullets' lips pucker up and skim
the surface

lacing it

with blisters of small bubbles.

Clodius intercepts my gaze   trained on him:

Suddenly he shakes the water from his hand,

'Pompey replaced Lucullus' command.

… But that's not why I'm home …'

No?
The word on the streets is: he stirred up Lucullus' ranks:
Mutiny has a cost: they lost
some territory to Mithridates who fled to Colchis

But I'm not about to mention this

You heard about Cataline?

Clodius seethes:

'This is Rome …
Cicero won't get away with
putting citizens to death …

But first I need to know
Everything …

What do you say?
You and I …

Pay to break Cicero's seal …'

Intercept his letters?

I can't believe the undertow I feel

An exhilarating thrill

COMPETITION

'I heard from Calpurnia
That today a well-endowed *vir* was
applauded in the baths.'

Metellus stifles a yawn,

'*Vanitas!*
That … my dear Clodia
Is the length some men will go to.'

'At least …'
Resentment festers in my unsaid words:

Since Metellus became *Praetor*
What is counted, what counts
Are *denarii*; only these rise
before him, in meticulous silver columns.

I don't care if it is late
I send a slave
To ask the fellow's name —

The length I will go to —

That sort of dedication
Shouldn't go
Unrewarded.

PRICKS

Damn these factional politics:
My hair's already grey, my pulse is racing,
My face is tingling and I suspect, red,
To top it off, today, at Speaker's Assembly, they hollered:

'You want to run as *Praetor*, Metellus?
Maybe you should 'take in the pin', and
preserve your energies for
Public
Performance!'

Command an army and at least you know
Which direction
To expect battle from.

At home Clodia says I always pick arguments:
If she were behaving
As she should be behaving,
I wouldn't need to remind her.

She expects me to stand to roll-call;
She's voracious,
There's no end to her appetite,
Says I need the root of that orchid, *saleb*
To revive me, to bring me to rise:

Every honest man knows
It's *these* distractions lead to the neglect of public affairs.

SECOND CATILINARIAN ORATION

'In Cataline's bands
We see all the gam-blers, and adult-er-ers,
All the un-clean and shame-less citizenry'

So the oratory begins,
Cicero waving his instructive finger before us
As if the Senate were full of children:

'His witty del-i-cate boys have learned —
Not to love and be loved —
But to use a dagger and to administer poison!

If they are not driven out; if they don't die;
If Catiline does not die; then I warn you,
The school of Catiline will take root in our Re-pub-lic!'

Cato agrees: 'Let me remind you, honourable men,
That the prisoners had planned to make war on Rome!
Three nights ago – that would have been the fateful night-
Lentulus and Cethegus in the lead,
Statilius and Gabinius ready to give the go ahead,
Twelve of their men would start simultaneous fires
In twelve chosen districts; hoping
Chaos would ensue, so someone willing to
brutally slay Cicero at his door —
none other than the pumped-up-Cethegus —
could spill his blood!
Panic, raging fire and still
more bloodshed! Sons of *nobiles* told
to murder their fathers!
Oh it would have been a right
bloody time, were it not for Cicero!

Were it not for Cicero

Convincing the Allobroges to infiltrate
the conspirators.'

Cato nods his head at several other Senators and me
As he looks about the Curia; to make the oratory personal:
Next he'll invoke my name.

'Good thing they told him
everything
Marcus Cae-lius!
How the envoys would cross the Tiber on the Via Flaminia, at Pons Mulvius to the north.

Were it not for Cicero …
The Praetors Lucius Valerius Flaccus and Gaius Pompinus
Wouldn't have known
to lie in wait upon
That very bridge!'

Cato, breathless, mops his brow:
'So Senators, now what's to be done?'

A volley of responses from the optimates: Pigeons scattered by slingshot.

'I say imprison him *in perpetuo!*'

There's a gasp, and someone mutters,
'For life? That's intolerably severe!'
'And keep him *where exactly*?'
'Too risky!'
'What about a penalty?'
'A fine?'
'Confiscation of property?'

'Loss of citizen rights?'
'Banishment?'

'A sentence of imprisonment? There's no such thing!'

'The prison's only temporary safe-keeping …'

'Safe?
What's safe -
with so many of his sympathisers still at large -
other than a doubtful assumption?'

Caesar chips in,
'In accordance with custom,
Our condemned should go into voluntary exile'

'To scuttle more of the cockroaches into le-gions
of rank and file?'
Cicero's incredulity is plaintive.

Cato, man of reason, steps into the fray,
'Easy to say, Caesar …
Other crimes can be punished
when they have been committed …
But with a crime like this,
unless you take measures
to prevent its being committed,
it is too late; once it has been done,
it is useless to invoke the law:
when a city is captured,
its defeated inhabitants
lose everything.

Whether you agree or not with Cicero
what matters most — Catiline's trial was salutary —

Two thirds of his troops in Etruria
deserted him immediately!'

CICERO

I can't stand that Clodia,
So I'm at a loss to explain these imaginings:
Like flashes of lightning across the Gaulish Plain
6th hour of the night
1st hour of the day

Her stately head
Her commanding shade
Her breast lifting breath
Her radiant face
Her proud cheeks
Her ribald speech
Her defiant chin
Her fulsome lips
Her lithesome limbs
Her shapely calves
Her softened soles
Her manicured toes

Each time a partial embodiment:

Were each piece wedged on a stake —
In scenes worthy of Gaul — I'd understand: Revenge.

It's disingenuous to think my motives pure;
I believe that: But, if this is — dare I even say it — *lust*?
Then what?
What then?

REVELATION

As I enter the *exedra,* Clodius waves a papyrus scroll:
'It's from Cicero to Atticus!'
His flapping hand beckons me to the space
Next to him; our ritual meeting place
On the fish pond's rim

Clodius' turn to read:
Like a nervous quail, his head bobs over every word.
He leans toward me, eyebrow raised:

'Well, well, well.'

I try to peer around the mound
of his fleshy hands, but he stands and skitters off
Like a lizard caught napping on the sunlit paving stones

'Ha!' he guffaws,
            and fixes me in his gaze:

'Well, well, well.'
            His face beams,
                        'Aren't *you* fanning his flames!'

I snatch the letter.

'If Cicero only knew it was you, Clodia,
            scrawling epigrams here and there,
Amusing all and sundry,
Making him the laughing stock of Rome …

… He'd regret slighting you
            with that impertinent term,
                                    Poetria!'

I’ve read enough:
Contemptuously I let the sprung cylinder recoil

To the marble floor

Where it drum-rolls its own significance

CLODIUS' GANG

We've all been embroiled in sex scandals;
All been on the receiving end
Of a chorus of jeering and abusive sloganeering

All choose to ignore
That chanting abuse is akin to murder
In Roman law

It's time: I signal to the mob gathered
Before me in the *Rostra*

A hush falls; time to show my mettle:

With a forefinger, I touch the side of my head

Who swims inside his scent bottle?
I implore my men, flounce a little,
Grab my toga and shake out the folds

Whose hands flap around like a *chiroptera*
I demand to know

Each word precise and slow
'What's the name of the sex-mad General?'

'Louder!'

'What's the name of the sex-mad General?'

My gang, like a trained chorus
Scream out the answer in unison and glee

'Pom-pey!' 'Pom-pey!' 'Pom-pey!'

SPEAKERS ASSEMBLY

I'm railing against the *improbi*
in the open air of the Forum.

Suddenly up springs Clodius

'Why should you wait for applause, Cicero,
When you're so good
                    at giving yourself
                                        a hand!'
The crowd roared with laughter

A few roughs had no qualms
In giving gesture to
                    the double pun.

So you see, Tiro, he's taken to giving me
A public bloodletting, in drips and drops.
It's not just the speech-making at every meeting,
He uses my name to stir up ill-feeling;
Even the honest men are yielding to his pleas.

I'm told gangs are in formation.

Can you imagine?
Organised gangs?
Those roughs?
The lot can't even piss straight!

TREATMENT

Metellus is in Cisalpine Gaul:

While he commands the Province

My desire's dressed up

With nowhere to go, again.

I'm even tiring of my *olisbos*

My reliable leather-bound friend.

62 – 61BCE

LEFT HANDED

I overheard mother
telling father

'I don't understand:
The omens were good on our wedding night –
You carried me over the threshold,
You made sure to step with your right …

His brother turned out fine-
How could *he* be so
unlucky?'

Swathed in cloth
My arms and legs tied to sticks
I couldn't move

Eventually my parents freed my right arm
To make sure I grew up
Right handed

Unlucky
Unlucky
Eagles flying across the sky

I fought against that misfortune:
First in the family to make the Senate;
A *novus homo*, a new man.

So understand Tiro, why I'm vexed:
Is there such a thing as inner crookedness?
How else to explain my incorrigible
left hand; today it sprang out
to greet someone.
Again.

CROSSING

Beside me now in the *cubiculum*, Clodius bites a wad:
The *alipilus* depilates him quickly, with precision; before long
 Clodius is pimply as a plucked quail.

I ease the *peplos* gently over his head,
fasten it at shoulder line; the two large pins of gold
depict a scene: a cat stalks unsuspecting birds;
                    Clodius intends to do the same.

I position the bone hairpins in his elaborate wig
Moisten ash to darken his brows and line his eyes

A flute girl is born:
'Pulcher!' I tease my brother: *'Pretty boy!'*

INTERCEPTED LETTER FROM CICERO

I expect you have heard, Tiro

An unknown man disguised in women's clothing
In-truded into the *Bona Dea* festival —
Into Cae-sar's
own
residence —

The national sacrifice, dis-rupted;
The Vestals had to repeat the en-tire ceremony.

A dis-honourable
and therefore mis-erable business!

Quintus Cornificius raised the matter in the Senate,
The Vestals and the Pontiffs pronounced the act sacrilegious,
And the consuls, by senatorial decree, promulgated a bill:

Well! Then Cae-sar sent Pompeia notice of divorce:
The very sug-gestion
that it was at her request!

Who would be so au-dacious? : I hear you ask:
For sure they do not know:

But who, except Clodius, is pretty enough to wear women's dress
And has a flyblown reputation to match it?

HARD TO SWALLOW

'Jupiter's balls!
I knew this would happen!'

Cicero throws his rigid, knuckle yellow
Hands up before me:

My momentary flinch sets him pacing the *atrium*

'You mark my words, Tiro,
Clodius bought them off! That *im-probe*
Up and walked away. Walked away! From the Sen-ate!'

His voice squeaks like a pulled cork
'Just … like …'

The back of his right hand strikes his left palm,
' … That!

And the cart that came before this horse?
That dis-reputable jury - more maggoty than a carcass!
Corruption: how it stinks in the nostrils of mother earth!'

His hand sweeps up like a startled thrush:
On the near side of his thumb, what's that? A flap of skin
flags his unhinging; the epitome of everything
he must gnaw at in frustration.
He wrests it off; sees my forehead pucker
with consternation; resolves to grind it only once or twice
before he spits it to the marble floor.

'You walk above ground,' I placate him, 'leave it for the worms!'

But just like the thumb he tucks into a closed fist;
There's no stifling the sting.

RIGHT HAND MAN

I'm in the Senian baths, of all places, Cloelius, when
 - talk about a lack of discretion -
Some would-be assassin comes up to me, 'psst, Clodius …', and wants
Weapons. Quite specific; a *parazonium* in a scabbard, and clubs;
No questions asked, and all by nightfall

I shift along the rows of wooden benches
In case somebody's listening:
There's the sound of lapping water
Acrid smoke from the furnaces
The heated floor, the wisps of steam
That musky mildew smell;
But no conspirators as far as I can tell

So, with a callous laugh I nod to
the phallus-shaped *fascinum* around his neck

'What need have you of weapons?'

Only then
I note his gaunt face, scraggly beard,
narrow hips and pigeon chest:

'On second thoughts, come back today with payment;
Exchange takes place outside the city gates.'

No names mentioned, Cloelius,
    But his arse is woollier than a *flokati*
I'd recognise that *culus* anywhere again;

The weapons, that's where you'll come in;

This is a job for my right-hand man.

BROKEN SPELL

I wake unwell, my troubles eight-legged, crepuscular;
the night before the Ides of March.

A dark shape fills the brazier-lit space;
Not man not beast
It writhes and groans

But then I recognise the groan

The beast dissects into two selves
And the one, small, brown, a faun,
Folds forward
Suddenly, as if ripped from flesh
And the other, hirsute and gruff, repositions
its hoof, hooves, hands
Upon the narrow hips

Silently I watch
Until the beast is still
While the full
Implication grips me
In its own insistent coitus

Now I realise
what

'I want to imagine'

means: Metellus wants *the fig.*

THE MORAL HIGH GROUND

'You've adopted the Palatine position!'
                                        scolds Clodius,
as he flicks several small pebbles
plonk! plonk! plonk! into the pond,

'Metellus is a desert waste;
Perhaps you should be glad.'

He lines new pebbles up
for a subsequent attack. *Plonk!* A struck eel
shimmies toward the shady recesses
of the pond's rim. I can't help but grin;
He did this as a young boy —
Long before he wore the crimson banded toga *pretextae*
Of adulthood —

A sudden tingle in my cheek, a rivalry
I choose to forget: and an acknowledgment:

He always could pick his targets.

I remind myself: Metellus is within his rights.

Clodius reads my vacillating thoughts:
'So he wants the fig? It's not as if it involves citizen youth.'

Several pebbles *plonk* before
The old saying spills its mealy guts:

It's not about him.

'What then?'
I can't explain.
Nor can Clodius find the foothold to my mind.

61BCE

WORKING THE ROOM 1

The invitation read: The lady Clodia requests
Your presence. Caesar in attendance.

So I've Caesar to thank that Garda's crested waves
Deposited me in Rome, and let it be known, on the Clivus Victoriae —
The oldest and most exclusive residential address
Fifty feet above the forum, on the edge of the Palatine —

Caesar's headed for great things:
And what a head; small with huge dark eyes,
Fair hair; a good sort; could almost fancy him;
Elegantly dressed, his tunic fashionably fringed,
Loosely worn: He's taller than I recall, but I couldn't forget that slim
Supple body; it may be older but it's still emanating
Ripples of nervous energy

Remembers me:
From a visit to my fathers …
Futuo, in that case …
Father sends his regards

Move on Catullus: It doesn't do
To do father's friends:

Pity: so refreshingly urbane.

WORKING THE ROOM 2

Ah! The ethereal aroma of roasted poppy seeds
Leads me through a regal vestibule
to a high-ceilinged hall.
Yet another introduction: Manlius Torquatus, liberal nobility.
Dabbles: Poetry, Law, Epicurean Philosophy.
My eyes flit noncommittally. With company this dry
I'll have to rely on the appetisers
in the *gustatio* to stimulate my appetite.

Saved: Tender asparagus shoots to dip in olive oil,
Roll in a little heap of sea salt

Temporary respite: Lucius Valerius Flaccus, born for his belly —
Can't decide whether to talk or eat —
Greets me, mouth full of *beccafia,*

'Ah, Catullus!' *altogether too familiar*,
A fleck of pastry on his puffy bottom lip
Flutters with each burst of breath.

Since Furius,
my old–er man
left me …

I chew the crunchy heads of some spicarae
… *and for a pimp* …
The truth is:
I don't give one sesterce for old men's concerns …

A few weeks of
strengthening foods and bulbi has finally raised my pecker …
I've a young man's predilections once again:

So up yours old men!

WORKING THE ROOM 3

Hold on, who's that sweet-looking boy,
                                        circulating with a laden tray?
Silver cups of expensive spiced wine … suddenly I've a thirst!

He glides to where I sit near the *fontes.*
Long limbed and lean, he towers above me like a huge fig tree

I'm Romulus
                                        I flirt aloud, frivolous with risk
Let me drink wine dripping from the whole laden breast!

I extend a hand:
Pinch-lipped, he promptly fills it with a cup.

Tight-arsed Allobroge
My mind's made up: Time to bow out gracefully

Disappear from my sight or you'll rupture me!

                                                                        Fortunately
he obliges: Move on Catullus; any fool can see
                                                                    For the moment
                                                                    he's not handy.

CAPTIVATING

'In every season, the first hour of the night
Is the most beautiful hour in Rome.'

Our host sweeps like a peacock's tail
Through a colonnaded archway to the *exedra:*

With a graceful hand Clodia motions
Here, to the fishpond's sensual statuary
There, to a host of sparrows flying free below mesh
Here, to the fountain's effervescent bubbling
There, to a *sentinella* of towering cypress trees

The shimmer of her *stola* opaque in the light;
Her luminous creamy throat offered
Up to the cerulean sky, to the
redolent night air.

Catullus, I chide myself, you're besotted, giddy;
Is it lust she's loosed? You're jiggling like *sesterces* in a purse.

WORKING THE ROOM 4

Opening like a gift, a space on a *lectus* in the *triclinia*
Allows me to recline;
                                        the early summer wine I imbibe,
White, with anise and a few drops of attar of rose
Should, but can't, cool my constitution:

 If Clodia would just look at me
                                                  the gift would be a prize:
Her long dark lashes usher my gaze
Into the emerald pools of her eyes.

Propped on my left elbow, I realign my toga
To conceal the rising in its fold;

Nearby, on the gold dish, olives - fleshy *Halmades*;
                                                            The extent of my reach.

NAME DROPPING

'The Claudian name's inscribed …

On the bronze code …
On the Twelve Tables on the arches …
On Rome's first aqueduct …'

But of course! I say as Clodia recites her credentials,
Sarcasm tingeing my tone.
She's pretentious; I'm irked; yet I'm holding my breath:
Each sweet grape she plucks from the bunch
Hovers before my lips:

On the first Appian Way?
Remarkable …

And on the august consul list?
Let me guess,
scores of times …

… So one of your forebears must
have been a vestal virgin?

One of your forebears
was

a vestal virgin.

Suddenly my face drains:
My credibility plummets to my knees.

I see.
What?
The fool I've been.

Her jewellery carries more weight
venustas
doctrina
more bearing
more distinction
than to dazzle my desire

Now she eyes me, warily,

'Your accent, Catullus … it's from the north?'

means
'You come from beyond the Po'?'

means
'You're a Provincial …'

means
I'm *so* out of her league.

LOADED

So, you're the daughter of A. Claudius Pulcher …

Her eyes widen,
It's the leeway I need

What I don't understand
is why you
haven't
told
me
You're the wife of Q. Metellus Celer …

Suddenly her bright marbles reflect me
small and distant;
down-sized for my indiscretion.

I anticipate a slap; an expression
of disdain: Instead she retorts: 'I guess you could say …
                    I like to play
around with
                    nomens and *cognomens*.'

My breath catches in a cough.

POETASTER

'So!' Clodia's tone pulls me upright. 'You're a poet?'
The last syllable drops away like my jaw.

It's risky, but I take a tentative guess
At her intentions:
You'd like *me* to read my verse?

'Recite' she corrects me, 'for the guests.
Over there.'
It's more a command than a request.

She points to the east of the fishpond.
Bordered by tall cypress trees
stands a small stage with mosaic walls;
Its fragments of gold and lapis lazuli
strike like flint in the twilight

'So Catullus, can you spare a pentameter for me?'

The perfunctory delivery and directness in her tone
Silences a huddle of nearby senators

I draw in a slow breath, glance at the half-submerged *clepsydra*
in the pond: time's up.

I check I have an audience for my riposte:
Well …
I must say
You've inspired me
To make the Alexandrian love epigram
very
            personal.

Clodia glares until the smirking senators turn,
Then her eyes scan me coolly, shoulder to shoulder,
as if to locate a vulnerable spot in a bronze shield.

'We shall see, Catullus
                    If you can live up to expectations ...
We shall see.'

SMITTEN

When my mind begins to draft love's composition
My body becomes captive.

'Suns can westward sink again to rise
But we…
But we…
But we…'

Unless I can insert the right words
in the right places, I'm *mollis.*

Quare id facis implores my *Imperator,*
Why do you do this?
My slave answers *nescio;* I don't know

It's barely a week since I met Clodia
And my poem's short by several lengths

My pathetic knob shares its sentiment

GARGANTUAN

As promised, Atticus, my report on the exceptional *munera*
Held four days before the *nones* of *September*.

...

Pompey's conquest of Africa
brought back strange beasts —
You know the ones,
Large ears that flap and fan like palm leaves —

The sound these beasts make is hollow, and resonates
Like the horns that signal *let the games begin*:
I can tell you though, twenty of them,
all at once,
bring forth an incredible din;

The spearmen attacked twenty such beasts:

Lined up and released their spears in lots.

The beasts stamped their protest in the sand,
Full thickness of foot, until the dust rose up;
But, gargantuan as they are, they could not
Be lashed into a rage of bravery: only one
separated from the herd and charged repeatedly;
Each of the others gathered the young. With one long,
bristled, probing trunk, they tucked the calves between
their legs. Though the rattle of spears rained down on their backs;
They remained; Collective armour:
This behaviour, from beasts?

Needless to say, they succumbed to the will of men
And knelt, heavy, tiresome deaths;

The calves were left standing, surrounded
by the humungous corpses.

Then as volley upon volley began to silence them
Their trumpeting dissolved in bleats

And like newborns to teats   they fell
              to their meagre ends, with little pageantry

…

Yet having said all this, Atticus, it's the citizenry who puzzle me.
Not only did they cover their ears. They began to weep:
In fact, they wept profusely. It was on for young and old, *matronas*
and *viros!*
Sight unseen, hard to believe;

Dead beasts: they've seen them many times before.
And many times before, this entertainment — as you know —
Afforded them
                           much pleasure

Yet the death of these beasts moved them
                                                  deeply

More than the mastery of the spearmen

The crowd began to thin, and as they made to leave
They hurled abuse, not cheers, at Pompey their General!
Yes, you read right, no need to rub your eyes:
I Cicero, mislead you not: They turned on '*quiff and smirk'!*

…

I leave you to consider this final thought:

Fourteen statues flank the theatre —
Each conquered nation is represented here —

But where is the thrill of blood lust?
Where is all the talk of war?

LEARNING THE LASH

'I be-lieve you've met
              Gai-us Val-er-ius Catull-us.'

I nod, 'The provincial … from Verona.'

My armpits register a sudden sweat.
A colonnade reassures the path ahead,
But where will this questioning lead?

'Savvy at networking the *patricios*, I hear.
Spends all his leisure with
the consular families.'

Unexpectedly my answer reaches its target.

'Jove
only
knows,
Cae-lius!
That
      syc-o-phant
burrows into their closed circle
like a hare!'

I veer past a *taberna vetus*
where the owner, an unscrupulous loan shark
leans sullenly in the doorway

Safely out of earshot, head high, I continue,
'I hear… he's showing what a roman tongue   can do.'

There's a contemptuous pause
Cicero punctuates with a crick of his neck.

Where have I gone wrong?

He turns on me curtly, dismissively.
'Oh yes, by Jove, he's elo-quent,
In hatred, as in love;
But don't tell me what you
hear,
Cae-lius,
Or you'll try my patience …'

Abruptly he halts, rigid with rage;
His voice has reached pitch:
He wrestles it down for better effect,
Resets his words in time with his pace.

'This …
woman …
about whom
Catullus writes …

high birth beauty wealth health wit
and
conspic-u-ous intelligence?'

Cicero pauses so long
I'm inclined to comment,

But then he pulls his stumpy body upright,

'It's …'
The words squeak out of stranglehold,
'Quite an endowment … wouldn't you say?'

Again, a long pause,

But now I'm sure
I'm not meant to answer.
I lease my villa from Clodius,
Whose sister Clodia, is, *well, friendly*, with Catullus.

'Any-one we
know?' he glares.

Suddenly my step feels longer than my leg.

NO HALF MEASURES

‘The name is *Lesbia,’*
                I shrug, noncommittally.
‘But as far as Catullus is concerned, she lives
Only in his poems.’

‘Cae-lius,’ Cicero chortles, ‘my dear Cae-lius,

And you … want to be … an orator?’
A rhetorical question he chooses to answer
Imperiously as a scorpion:

‘Then you have much to learn,

For she lives …

You will see …

She lives.’

ASKING FOR IT

'Tell me about the *Claudii* …'

Manius Graecus' bronze stirring wand slips from his hand,
clangs to a halt on the rough-hewn stone

'Catullus…
Eh, you don' wan' to know …'

He bends to where the wand lies, stuck with wisps of hay,

Returns to the task of his cellar tour
— our talk of wine —

Taps a nearby wooden lid,
'This one … grapes from …
Just you wait 'til you taste't …'

Noting my expectant look, he sighs deeply,
As if the details personally pain him;

A chuff of garlic plumes from his breath:
our earlier meal of pottage
and pork sausage.

'During the Civil Wars *eh* …
Appius Claudius was banished by Cinna'

He runs a wine stained hand through his rippled black hair

'Beats me how …
That family must have lived on the smell of *garum* …

Until Sulla …'

He registers my quizzical look

'His property *was* returned …
But by then … *o po' po'* … three daughters and three sons *solo*

… The mother long dead …

… The eldest Claudia had married Marcius the *Consul*
Before the worst disaster

… Then Claudia the younger married Luculus …'

Which left … Clodius and Clodia?

He nods, and stretches,
Placing both hands in the small of his back

'To … to … , *eh,*
Let's just say … to devise a life of their own'

His mouth pulls to one side
Like a horse that resists the rein

'There were some ugly rumours *eh* …'

I'm sure there's a logical explanation, I offer,
Too forcefully   I realise
                        too late

Suddenly he peers at me,

'Ti kano?'

What am I doing?
Legions might ask, but I'm not about to tell

But then legions don’t know me as well
                                        as Manius

‘*Yiati*?’
‘Why?’

The question whistles like an arrow through trees.

Faced with my silence Manius groans.
He needn’t hear another word.

‘In love?

Again *eh*?’

His palm strikes the baseline of his hair,

‘*Vir,* you’re a walking *haemorrhagia*.’

QUICK LEARNER

As we reach the Shrine of *Janus*
Cicero pivots round to face me:

'In oratory Cae-lius, you learn to look both ways.
You learn to cal-cu-late your risk.'

You have to admire the man's flawless timing.

I take a deep breath and follow his advice,

'What about the risqué verse
Scrawled on the baths and urinals …
I hear it's making the senatorial class
squirm …'

'Pfff,' Cicero exhales, looking away, 'Goss-ip and slander.'

Then his broad eyes, twinkling perniciously, pinion mine:

'Look. I don't per-son-ally
                    be-lieve
                                    that Clodia poisoned her husband —
Or that she's had, shall we say,
                                    Im-prop-er relations with Clodius —'

To this he adds, after a sudden chortle,

                                    'But le-gions do.'

His left arm tightens across his protesting gut:

He's determined to hear my next move: Am I in?
A quick reckoning — Career in the Senate?

Or peppercorn rent? Clodius' condition:
Catullus and Clodia meet at his place
any time they please —

A no-brainer.
I look him straight in the eye.

Flamma fumo est proxima

Where there's smoke …

It's not bleating praise

But I register a flinch of approval in the smirk on Cicero's face.

VALENTINE

It's *Aprilis*, Venus' month, a reason to give
Lovers' gifts. Not that I need a crystal ball, ivory dice
To gaze into or to roll. I can take all
I want: From Catullus' pouch.
He'll vouch for my sparrow's safe return: He'll recall
my pet my plaything in my lap or at my breast
And wish himself wings
And desire like bird: fern; forest; nest.

60 – 57BCE

BETWEEN MEN

We arrive at the *Campus Martius*, the Field of Mars:
Building's begun on the site of Pompey's planned
huge
stone
theatrum

Cicero ignores me, harps on about Clodia,
Of late, his favourite oratory

'... She's devoted to vain display
... spends all her time in the company of *infames*
... not the model *matrona*, nor the model wife;
... you don't see my
Terentia
leading a reckless wasteful life ...

Metellus should've given her
the full length of his concern!'

He extends an arm forward in a closed fist
And lets a whistle skid through his teeth;

In the thin and bitter line of his lip
I recognise a man whose appetite is
Barrelled up

'You raise her name so often that
I'm starting to think ...'

I wink at him
and copy his arm and whistle action

'given half a chance ...'

His face blusters; it's as if a clutch
Of startled birds was flushed out from a bush.

I raise a hand to stifle his mounting objection

'Of course,
That's strictly between us …'

And then, to raise the stakes, I add,

'Since you and I have shared,
Excepting her,
So much …'

FLOODING

'It's a low-lying plain,'
I challenge Cicero,
'How does Pompey think he'll prevent
The *Campus Martius* from inundating
When the *Tiberis* rises again?'

Cicero bends and picks up a leaf, but will not answer me —
Nor has he —
The whole return journey —

Privately I'm prepared to consider:
Perhaps I went too far?
I merely pointed out
That, for a while —
In fact, since his return from exile —
His relations with Terentia had been 'strained'.

I shrug my shoulders:
It *is* public knowledge;
How can it not have sunk in?

The entire walk back from the *Campus Martius*, silent;
The whole time looking at his leaf.

INTERCEPTED LETTER FROM CICERO: SOFT TARGET

'I hope you've got thirsty ears!'
Clodius calls
over the fountain's gentle pulse.

He strolls through the *exedra* towards me,
a *papyrus* half-unrolled in his hand;
it wilfully trails over spring blooms
inciting rise   from a siesta of flies

He props a sandalled foot on the pond's rim.
Strong; striking; ardent: *Ehi tó chárisma,* I smile to myself:
With his wild black mane; his long proud nose
Indeed   the gods have graced him

Clodius strikes a pose I recognise: Cicero in oratory:

He thrusts out a shortened neck; winks at me,
'Cicero needs
a thor-ough-ly
trust-worthy
mess-en-ger …

I can't im-a-gine
why?'

Tears of laughter pool in my eyes
He's mastered the nasally twang, the odious tone:

'Of course …'   Clodius begins to read,

'He wouldn't want   his   letters

such as they are …

… to get into

a strang-er's hands.

So he won't write in his own name …

Or use his seal …

And he plans to invoke some
se-cret
code …
He'll call
him-self,
Lae-lius,
and
Att-icus,
Fu-rius.'

Laughter ends the pillory.

Clodius loses his composure,

collapses next to me on the pond's rim.

A chorus takes over with perfect timing:
Like *Subura* gossips, loquatious sparrows dash to this spot and that,
trills teeming through the jasmine filled air;

Heads together wings a-quiver beneath the hemp net.

CLODIUS ADOPTED BY A PLEBEIAN

You won't believe your eyes Tiro, read on.
It's Ceres Day: I've just come out of the Antium district
and joined the Appian Way at Tres Tabernae
And who comes along but young Curio
On his way from Rome
And have I heard the news:
Clodius … standing for Tribune?

Tribune, I say, How's that?

Seems he approached the *triumvirs:*
Caesar, as *Consul* and *Pontifex Maximus,*
moved the *lex curiata de Arrogatione*
and Pompey assisted as *Augur*

By this Clodius legally became the adopted son
of the Plebeian, Publius Fonteius.
Now Clodius takes the *praenomen*
'Publius'
'for the people, of the people'

He's already been Quaestor so he's had a taste of the finance
But if he gets up as Tribune of the plebs
He'll have wide constitutional powers, oh yes,
and that's not the worst of it! If he can veto
any piece of public business, including laws and senatorial decrees
and initiate his own,
Can you imagine?
The shit will really go down!

SUMMER ELECTIONS

'Caesar says we need a dignified building to house elections …
Not this … *ovile*,
                    this sheepfold …'

Clodius scans the flat stretch of land of the field of Mars
          and wipes his brow.
The eleventh hour, and already the day is heavy with heat
          and the dragonflies' sonorous hum.

We watch the voters being ushered into roped-off *comitiorum*:
thirty-five for the *comitia tributa*
eighty for the *comitia centuriata*
thirty for the *comitia curiata*

'First we separate the sheep from the goats, Clodia …

          Then we make them bleat …'

                              A wide grin pleats Clodius' face

I glance across to the pons: where, in order of superiority,
the voters, the *suffragatores*,
go up one side of the platform, then down the other
                                        with the uniformity of ants

Midway, ready to receive each *tabella suffragium*
Cloelius, holding the urn

'Where's the rest?' He knows I mean his gang:

'Bribing votes in the comitia …
Buying votes at the crossroads from the poor …'

From off the Apulian mountains there's a sudden gust
of scorching
wind

My hand flies up to resist its pummelling
This heat!
Time to head down to Baiae …
There'll be red mullet; leverets in the leporium; plenty of honey …
Perhaps you and Fulvia can join me … after …

I lower my tone

The hirelings, Clodius …
Are they …
reliable?
I squint up at the multitude of faces
refracted in the hazy sun:
On each one the hint of a smile

Clodius scans his ranks magisterially
before giving an adamant reply

'Num mus uni fidit antro?
Does a mouse
rely
on just
one
hole?'

BESTIARI

The *bestiarius* looks from one l*eo* to the
then glances at his   next,
                                  one   four in all,
                                          dagger.

'He's got reason to worry…'

Manius runs a hand along the back of his neck

'Each beast *eh*
                                  weighs more than four men.'

It's not like I need convincing

But having grown up on the Sirmio Peninsula
I've never seen a show.

What's the *ordo propria*?

Manius squares his *kouroi* thighs
as if he himself might wrestle the beasts.

'Never applaud what is not good, Catullus …

The bestiarius must kill with integrity …

A competent performance with a difficult animal …
eh that shows *fortitudo*!'

Manius' nostrils flare
revealing short black tufts of bristly hair

'But he must control his moves
Not too much this —'

His sandalled feet
like flummoxed bees

zickzack

this way
and that.

Manius stops with a cough in the rising dust

Won't he run?

Manius recoils
'To run … Catullus?
O po' po' …'

His words lunge at me
'That would be shameful … spiritless …'

Suddenly there's a roar from the crowd

'Incredibile!'

The bestiarius has thrown himself around a beast's mane

A flick of wrist;
he draws his blade round its throat.

The fur parts in a thick crimson wad.
The lion falls
on

its
back
lands
on
the
bestiarius

who exhales with a honk.

A single squiggle of red
wriggles away
from his mouth's jubilant smirk.

Mirabile est?
I implore Manius, sufficiently impressed.

Yet his tight-lips
mirror those around us

nothing but frowns

As Manius rises he meets my confused face.
Hands on thighs he sits back down to explain:

'Most of all Catullus
the bestiarius should avoid
dishonour …'

His dark arm sweeps towards the arena
as if he were hurling refuse to a pit

'To die too soon …

through foolishness …'
He tuts,

'Ask any citizen, Catullus… and what does he recall?
That the bestiarius did not die well …

That his body cried out …

That he honked …

Like a goose.'

CLAUDIA OF THE EROTIC FRIEZE

Between courses
They have no appetite
For Sallust, the moralist

'those who indulge to excess
their appetites for food and drink
are susceptible to sexual temptation'

He hasn't got a bow for his arrows'
says Mistress Clodia,
'He hasn't even got a sling!
A toast to the *meretrix* in the erotic frieze!
She's being served a specialty dinner!
Let her speak of her appetite!

Gold raised, a laughing chorus
Imbibe her pleasure and sway.

She bids me speak. I speak.
Better I, than
Claudia of the marital scene
on the opposite wall,
framed by velvet drapes
like a virtuous *pièta.*

With her marjoram wreath, saffron veil
and matching yellow shoes:
those little golden feet
destined to remain
diminutive.

I'm in her face-I'm a poseur.
I'll trump the 'blurts' of Catullus' gossiping door.

TALLY

munera
The day's rewards

60 *leones*
40 *equi*
32 *elephanti*
30 *pantheres*
20 *muli*
10 *tigres*
10 *cervi*
10 *hyenae*
10 *giraffae camelopardi*
6 *hippopotami*
1 *rhinoceros*
10 *struthiocameli*
5 *ursi*
20 *cephi*

WOULD BE SACRED

'He who ruminates on the entrails of birds
Has us by the balls!'

Caesar rolls his eyes as he dismisses
the bevy of soothsayers from his pillared halls —

Whose findings of the 12th hour sacrifice include

'An enlarged spleen in one chicken
and a jaundiced duck's liver';

To which the sky watchers add

'Three hawks flew overhead' —

'How is it, Calpurnia,'
He appeals to me once they've gone
'That I govern innumerable men …
Yet I myself am governed by birds and thunderclaps?

… Sacred chickens …
Chickens are too stupid to know their counsel …
I for one think: when chickens eat, they're just hungry.

How I'd like to close the *auguraculum*
And cast off this burden
Of superstition and nonsense.'

I too, am sick of the *haruspices* —
        It's Romulus we have to thank
        For the divination of birds
        For the daily re-enactment of watching the skies —

Caesar punctuates his measured strides,

'Will Rome come to ruin if the gods are maleficent?
I'll save Rome with my wise counsel,
Not by poring over guts and turds!'

But I'm no longer registering his words:

I'm imagining days that are just days —
Neither lucky or unlucky —

Imagining birds that simply belong in the world of birds

OUTRAGE

'Clodia, I can't believe I've been indicted!'

Clodius is pacing the *exedra* like *pantherae* in a slave trader's cage

By whom?

'Titus Annius Milo.'

I glide out of harm's way find a dry spot on the fishpond's edge,
For what?'

'Employing violence …'

Why don't you speak with Appius?
He'll suppress the charge …

Clodius stares blankly ahead

'… Yes,'
he finally exhales a slow and measured breath

'And then I'll ransack his house in revenge …
I'll give him violent!
No more amateurs from the slums, Clodia …
well-armed,
well-trained men …'

But Clodius …
I protest,
That bestial laugh …
Milo's …
I gesture to my head with a wavering hand

Clodius registers: '*Insanus*?
Agreed …
But believe me …
Clodia -

that laugh

will end

on a blade …'

Clodius slits an invisible throat with a huge sweeping arm

I stifle a rising shudder,
Jove what a thought!

Clodius …
I place a hand on his shoulder,

I don't want you to come to harm …
He turns to me,
grinning broadly,

'Don't worry …
For every barker there's a bone …

Clodius winks,
… and I've got one big enough to silence
Milo.'

GRAIN DOLE

'It's true, Cae-lius,
the price has certainly risen very high …

But Clodius claims that the shortage is my …

How am I to blame?
For the flood?
For snow that melts in spring?
For winter rain?'

Cicero's pinched lip
takes refuge behind his silver cup

'How that … hyp-o-crite

can campaign the pop-u-lar vote …

with that mansion of his …

and his sister so proud of her rare fish …'

Cicero takes a sip. 'More wine?'
he offers without a drop.

I glance at the artworks around us in the *atrium*

Cicero stiffens,

'Alright … alright,

I don't de-ny my Corinthian bronzes are prized …

But let me tell you Cae-lius,

when Clodius' hirelings
flocked to the *Theatrum*
clamouring about the lack of food
like raucous squabbling gulls,

Clodius con-ven-i-ent-ly for-got

That the en-tire *Campus Martius*
— from the Tiber bend to the Pincian Hill —
bore a sli-my layer of debris and mud …

The *emporium*, you know, took the brunt of the flood …
So the grain sprouted green furze …

Like new beards on cleanskin boys!'

I grin cup empty

'But that, Cael-lius,'
Cicero scoffs,
'Is the bidding of gods!'

He downs the remnants of his wine

'This new law — free monthly distributions of grain —
Oh, it's a crowd pleaser all right!
To think … all citizens, even freedmen,
will collect five *modii* …

five *modii*!

Cicero's tone
crisp with censure,

'This grain business, Cae-lius,

It’s given Clodius the spur …

If someone doesn’t
pull
on
his reins …’

He clicks his fingers in the air

‘*Pffi!*

… it’s the end of the Republic as we know it!’

INTO EXILE

'I know it's late, Clodius …

It's Cicero …

He's slipped his leash.'

I recognise the grey tunic and dark
green cape of my henchman Cloelius
as he's ushered into the *vestibulum,*
his ruddy face, his curls, typically *Gaul*;
An ex-gladiator; his nose broken more
than once, his cheeks cracked like the veneer
of the Numidian-yellow marble floor.

As the news of Cicero's slinking departure
                                                                        dead of night
Begins to spread, I specify our job

'We'll surge along the Palatine,
Occupy his house, then reduce it —
                                                                      the most visible
public mark of his rank —
                                          block by block,
                                                                      to rubble …'

He holds up his willing hands
Fists the size of a stray dog's head
'Right,' he exclaims,

'I'll raise the mob.'

DIVERSION

'They say it lives in waterholes …'

Calpurnia leans toward me, wide eyed,
as a hippo bumps its way into the ring;
rotund as a scarab snorting and snuffling.

If her interest's feigned
I understand:
Caesar's gone to Gaul.

The beast stops and yawns.
'Take a look at its yellow swords!'

Calpurnia peers at its jaws, opened wide:
marvels at the puckered rows of skin inside

When the hippopotamus burps long and loud
Calpurnia titters; her peacock fan flutters
before her astonished eyes.

Calpurnia points out the constant *flick*
flick
flick of the beast's tiny ears
'It's disturbed by the noise …
Odd, isn't it?'
she adds, tapping my forearm,

'Given the extent of its own voice …'

I'm forced to admit she's right.

The beast's deep-throated reverb-
eration, a slow, coarse chuckle,

heh heh heh   *he-gh*

            like traders sharing dirty jokes in the marketplace

heh heh heh   *he-gh*

INTERCEPTED LETTER FROM CICERO: NUNINDAE

Believe me, the food shortages are far-reaching, Tiro …
On market days you should see the rustic tribes
that come in from the provinces …

Transtiberini   from beyond the Tiberis
Transmontani   from beyond the mountains

The ugliest of faces   and the widest of girths
They trudge to the baths

Sol-it-ary men   accompanied only by *canes*

The plump Umbrians bring shepherd dogs:
They've good noses for scent   and they're lively and keen.

The Transalpine Gauls bring sleek hounds
that clamour and bay when they sight a hare

But the fat-bellied Etruscans?
Their pomeranians take dainty steps   and won't chase a thing …
                                            All they do is whimper and cringe.

Funnily enough, Tiro,
whether it be Celtiberians …
dark and toothy Lanvinians …
Transpadani living on the north side of the Po' …
It seems only Milo
can withstand the smell under their armpits;
          You guessed it: he's on the lookout for new recruits.
But inside the baths
                    even the *strigiles* recoil
                                  at the backlog of sweat
                                                    and dirt!

56 – 52BCE

CROCODILUS

The beast's eyes blink
                                        blink
                                                        blink

in the noonday sun blazing down   on the arena

Calpurnia leans toward me

'I heard he begged   to be thrown from the Tarpeian Rock.'

Her amazed face: 'A criminal, Clodia! Begged!'

I turn to where he stands   completely still
                                        fear anchoring his legs

In the strange disquietude   the drone of flies

Calpurnia taps my forearm

'Do you think it's asleep?'
As if the criminal has heard off he creeps in tentative steps.

The beast opens one eye   emits a low hiss:
and without warning   sweeps the ground
                                        to within an ankle's width
                                        with a lunge, snaps his jaws around calf
                                        and foot

The criminal squeals   the rows of teeth a mouth of spears

The crowd around me roars: 'Stay strong in the legs!'
They mean 'stay and fight'   yet sense he will run.
How can a one-legged man run?

And yet he does.   In short erratic hops.

How can this long, laden beast move so fast?

Yet it does.   Its tail scuffs through rising dust.

I glance at Calpurnia
who sheepishly removes
the hand

squeezing my knee.   She looks at me, relieved
smiling   *at last*

A streamer of blood   spurts   across   the   sand.

The beast surges through

Sideswiping red mud

THE CIRCUS MAXIMUS

It's not what I would watch
by preference …
although you do have a point, Cicero —
When the freeborn gather here
they're less likely
to assemble at the Senate —

I look around me. From the wooden spectators' seats
where we stand, there's an unhindered view of the arena
its encircling water channel
added by Caesar
for protection

Remember the dedication of the temple of Venus Victrix, Cicero?
The day Pompey's elephants broke
the iron rails
and ran amok?

I lean forward, more to irritate Cicero,
than to imitate the crowd.

What a sight that was! I chuckle.
Up jumped the citizens! Frantic! Hoiking up their togas,
clambering
tumbling
over the wooden seats!

Cicero stiffer than a plank:
'We …
… are not
fascin-a-ted
with death,
its near-ness or avoid-ance.

We are fascin-a-ted

By vic-tor-y,

Cae-lius.

Vic-tor-y.'

There's a grisly

cruck

cruck

cruck

as Cicero cricks his neck

That'll be … *my turn* … *over.*

'Auronius told me the other day

Twenty-nine gladiators from German-ia

str-angled

each other

to avoid the ring …'

Cicero shakes his head ruefully

'The last one, Cae-lius …

Stuffed the bog brush

down his throat

on and on past the gag …

… until he suff-o-cated and died.

'The shame of it,' huffs Cicero,

'Be-haviour like that gives the games a bad name.'

CICERO TO ATTICUS

The news is this: Pompey arrived at his Cuman villa
on Shepherd's Day: sent a messenger to me straight away,
with his com-pliments. I've been here since,
discussing politics a good deal; and although my ears are still
ringing with his well-rehearsed maxims, on the whole he's been agree-
able.

Agreeably effu-sive, that is.

He told me about a visit from his Number Two.
Appar-ently Milo wastes no time getting straight to
                                                            the point.

                    'Several times Clodius's missed the blade …'
and
                    'You might as well stop nibbling

                    At what you must swallow …'

Let me tell you my jaw dropped.
I could see Milo: his legs propped apart,
thick as planks, shoulders slightly stooped,
those enormous hands clasped behind his back.

                    'That upstart of a fellow!' I exclaim.

Well! Pompey swishes round the room, taking his time to reply.
Finally he smirks, sips his wine, and says to me

                    'Cicero, on the contrary —

Nothing could have been more *apropos* —'

Essentially Atticus, Pompey's hands are tied.

It wouldn't be on his say-so …

But if Clodius should die?

It doesn't take three guesses to work out

Who's received favourably?

FLOGGING

'Sure, your brother's died …
Clodia's dumped you …
But *eh,*
            you don't have to roll over like a *canis.*'

Manius holds up a quintuplet of fingers
To rebuke me

That's all I need …
The mastery of his unspoken word —
The vice of his four fingers and thumb
Could pincer the legs of a songbird —

Cacat!   My sandal stubs an uneven marble block.
            I shrug off Manius's steadying hand
            and squint up at the *popina*, savouring its greasy-sweet smell;
                                                            rancid … just how I feel …

Manius pulls back, squinting at me:
                        Have I been eating *garum*?
                        Futuo!   He's noticed the edging to my teeth,
                                                a metallic bluish black —

No, something more astringent's in my mouth, the taste of lacklustre —
vino, veritas, culli, cunni — even friends no longer nourish me
and my poetry? meagre as grain

A sudden cramp in my gut:
I glare up at Manius, hands steadying my knees,

Ti Kano?
What?

'What the *futuo* am *I* doing?' he asks, incensed,
    'You're the one all saturnine and sullen.'

With a look of despair, he scuttles a cancrine hand
                                        through his hair,

'For Jove's sake, Catullus, with all the *mulsum* you've drunk
your thoughts are sunk in wine, you're wallowing like swine in it,

Vir…
    Can't you borrow some   wit?'

    His words run like a blade   ear to ragged ear

THE DEATH OF CRASSUS

'Fortes fortuna adiuvat!'

'Fortune favours the brave!'

Given we're on our way
                    to Crassus's wake

Even coming from Cicero

Fortune seems an   unfortunate   choice of word

'You know they poured molten lead
down Crassus's throat before sending his head
to the Parthian King?'

My tone rather more emphatic than I intend

Cicero's unfazed:
'Come now, Cae-lius …

The Parthians mere-ly
recognised
his taste
for money …'

'Cornelia his widow said …'

'*Oh* so she's given you the sob-story?'
                                        he implores me
                                                            one eyebrow raised
'Come, come, Cae-lius,
Don't be naïve,

Any
daughter of Scipio
knows
how to look after
herself …

She has plans to re-marry …
Oh yes,'
            he nods,

                        'Pom-pey …

                        Sure-ly
                                    you heard?'

His smug look.

The scorching in my gut.

Before us stands   Cornelia's door of bronze

'Ah Cae-lius,'
            he sighs like a old master,

            'desultor, desultor …
… the inconstancy of matronas …

… like *Circus* riders
            that leap from   horse   to horse …'

INTERCEPTED LETTER FROM CAELIUS TO CICERO

'Speak of the dog and pick up the stick!
Caelius, predictable
as ever …

Here, see for yourself,'
Clodius huffs.

I intercept the papryum as it topples
from his fingertips to the pond below
where bearded mullets, surfacing for air
skim the water's rim, precariously near

'Why … Cicero's not even out of the provinces
and the leech is ready to bleed him dry …'

The pithy palimpsest rustles open

As soon as you hear I'm elected
Please attend to that business of the pantheras

I look up at Clodius: No *if* or … *when …?*
Then the afterthought:
He wants leopards?

Clodius reclaims the scroll,

'*If* …
he's elected this summer to the *curule aedileship*

he'll have to give some of the official *ludos* …'

Clodius rolls his eyes,

'The price one pays for being a protégé.'

Wrist flexed, Clodius with taunting grin
pokes at a dragonfly   hovering above the pond.

It hurtles full speed into a trap:
the luxuriant mass of my black hair, swept-up
                  into a finely woven gold mesh net

Clodius doesn't notice   my arms flail   like thick eels

He's on-the-wing again, pacing the *exedra*, all het –up;

His perambulatory voice wavers,

'… couldn't even give him time to get to the province …'

he mutters   buzzing near my ear.

SERVITIUM AMORIS (CLODIA'S POEM FOR DELICATI)

Loosen the straps of your sandals

Of your own free will

Choose me

To bathe your feet

Trust me

To neglect the sponge

Dripping nectar on your toes

To tongue-trap each elusive drop

While I hold each foot,

As a gift,

Marvel the scandalous beauty of your thigh.

TRAGOEDIA

I'm visiting Fulvia while Clodius is away, overseeing the property in Bovillae.
Suddenly there's a clamour; a mob has formed near the gates.

What a rabble stands outside! I motion to the mob to step aside;
give them a wide berth.
A messenger is thrust forth:
It's Cloelius,

breathless

horseless

'Bovillae …' he pants …

A taper of blood hangs suspended
from his broken nose

I stare at his riding clothes — the heavy long sleeved tunic
usually cinched with a belt at the waist — now hanging free,
his woollen leggings torn and dirty
the smell of his armpits fetid as *tragi*

'Bodies … Clodia,'
Cloelius croaks like a raven,
'… scattered on the road …'

Where's Clodius?

Cloelius' eyes begin to close.
I shake his shoulder,
Tell me!

'Birria … threw a *javelin* …
… knocked him …. off his horse …'

I register Fulvia's gasp

and reach behind to clasp her hand

'Bring him inside the gates!' I command, and begin to turn,

But Cloelius slumps suddenly

like the derelict tenements in the *Subura.*

He's supported — just — by a scrawny freedman.

'*Eheu*!'

the freedman utters,

nose curled up,

'I think he's shit himself.'

Cloelius drops with a thud.

Get out of here! I bawl at him,

That's no way to treat the dead!

I turn to the others,

Take him home!

There's mumbling and shrugging: He has none.

I scowl at the lot of them,

Then take him beyond the Servian wall …

But even they've got scallops for balls.

They lift him gingerly

carry him off like a swine or a dog;

each of them holding a leg.

UP IN SMOKE

We pass, midway on the short-cut to the Forum, the Ramp:

'It's … the … *Curilia ... Hostilia* Caelius!'
pants Vettius, Cicero's wide-eyed informer,
gesticulating with such flourish that the limp
strands of his hair spatter me with sweat.

On his way to Cicero's no doubt
- a regular brown noser -
With the nickname 'Gladius'
'sword' or 'penis' neither of which he's got,
life's bound to be short.

In the distance echoing up from the valley:
solemn horns: the pipes' plaintive notes.

By the time I reach the Senate,
the wax tablets are molten;
Scrolls are unfurling like writhing snakes.

As night's own cape
descends upon the smouldering wood:
upon the broad marble steps, covered with soot:

A funereal feast: a banquet of black:
black beans, black sausages, black bread;
black cloths spread across tables,
dark blood-red wine;

All to honour Clodius: feasting and fires until well after nightfall.

CLODIUS' STATE FUNERAL

Hammering on the door:
It's Atticus, eleventh hour of night,
clamouring for
the
        wake.

The door creaks ajar

Atti-cus, must you wake the gods? Calm your-self *vir!*

I motion toward the open brazier,
With a clap of hands, order wine;
a decision I regret: my mouth's cordial line
pulls taut   in the plume   of his fermented breath

Atticus' words cascade like coals

'Clodius made   quite   an exit, Cicero,
Naked … except for a loincloth …
His wooden bier festooned with black,
Carried onto the Rostra,
Propped up for the crowd to see …'

He shrugs, as if he can't even believe
                                        his own commentary:

'The flames, Cicero,
                        swept   like invigorated fingers
over his flint skin   across his oiled torso   his long-limbed elegance,
teasing away his loincloth   licking his ears …
breathing heavily at his neck …

They sized up his   combustible   nature
Sidled up to him for a last,

lewd

dance.'

Atticus runs a tongue over his parched lips.

Hmm,

I take the opportunity to quip,

Sounds like
you should have
been
in his bed?

An attendant slides a cup into Atticus' hand

But he won't drink what he can't swallow

'No matter what you thought of him, Cicero,
… to be slain
at the hands of that
thug,
Milo.
To die,
like that …'

Atticus shakes his head,

'He was of the Claudii Pulchri,
No matter what …
He was one of *them*…

A fleck of spit flicks toward me like a wayward spark

Our eyes follow its trajectory

to where it falls short

'Cicero, you should have seen the mourners weep!
With guttural choking sounds they clawed at tangled hair …

As the bier reduced to cinders and ash …
As charred wisps fluttered into the air'

I glance up to where his gesticulating hands are threatening to *diskos*
the contents of the cup

'The grief was impossible to still;
Scuffles broke out; flames from the torches whipped
and snapped in the evening chill;
The cordons, as if rising to a charm, sinuously snaked away …'

'Hmmm'.

I stoke the brazier
viciously

until clouds of incense rise …

What's with him,
so damn an-i-mated,

dom-in-ating the oratory?

I snort back my displeasure: a sizeable gob.

Att-i-cus,
do you real-ly
ex-pect me
to renege?
I al-ways
thought Clo-dius was a dem-a-gogue:

Fifty sest-er-ces,
that's all it takes,
and one can seed a crowd,
or lead a mob …

Atticus looks at me with utter disdain,
thrusts his cup into my hand,

'*Ligo aima* …'

He shrugs,
capitulating nothing as he walks away,

'A little blood, Cicero

Can make a great stain.'

OPEN ALL HOURS (CLODIA'S POEM FOR CLODIUS)

You couldn't lead a life of virtue:
you walked among Plebeians and plotters
whose babbling brooks murmured
'murder':

Now your Book of the Dead
recommends
nothing
useful.

Wherever you go you'll start a brawl:
So take with you
your incendiary words,
your ravishing inflammatory smile;

Let your wild eyes
your monumental thighs
burn girls, burn boys.

MILO'S TRIAL

Even from the courtroom's marble *vestibulum*
Cicero's voice booms,

'Since the trouble on the Appian Way
Rome's been tigh-ter than a *culus*!'

Immediately there's a hum of disgruntled mutterings:

'You can say that again!'
'One fart and the whole armed guard hovers
'round the shit-hole, ready to
shut it down.'

No one envies Cicero this task:

To preside over these rival gangs
These bellicose ex-gladiators
and their street-wise counterparts
the shaggy-browed,
scraggly-bearded
rabble-rousers.

No one envies Cicero this task:
He'll need his head to save Milo's neck.

'As you're aware, this special court, this *nova forma,*
has been established for all cases arising out of the brawl
that led to the death of Clodius.

Today, before the temples are military guards —'
His face contorts to a wry grin —
'Halting our pro-gress … from prim-itive men …

All because *you* Milo, *and* Clo-dius,
Clubbed each other like bar-barians.

But be warned,
There's to be no violence, not here, today, nor any other day.'

Gazing at his thick-necked silhouette
I recall
Cicero once said

'To win, Caelius, you must
think of them
as straw men.'

That's why I know
Perhaps not without threat: But it will be done: He'll win

their stiff jawed consent.

MALEDICTION

We gather in the *atrio*
for the reading of Clodius' will:

Clodia mihi heres esto, it begins,
Clodia,   *oldest,*   *only …*
    beloved daughter   *be my heir …*

Appius looks across to the *impluvio*
    where fine rain glistens like spinnerets
        in the eleventh hour sun

There's an audible sigh: I for one know
        his propensity
            to digress:
Yet Appius clears his throat,
        lends renewed conviction
            to his emphasis:

'It seems Clodius believed Milo's threats …

… to have gone to the trouble
    of a will …

… to have lined up
    seven signatories,   adult, male   not blind or insane
        … to bear witness'

There's a sweeping sound as my sandal traces
    lines of mosaic in the marble floor;

    not blind, or insane,   but impatient.

'Atticus!'
    Appius assures me: he'll get to the point.

He glances around the room
with a troubled face,

'Unco trahatur'

'Let him be dragged!'
There's a gasp of shock
at Clodius' damnation legacy
for Milo
A rope
and a hook?

To be hung in the *carcer* like a common criminal;
To be hauled from its watery cell,
dragged off with a hook; a sodden, sullied sack

Despatched outside the city wall,
Splash! into the *Tiberis* downstream of the *Campus Martius.*

To intermingle with every imaginable refuse
in the weak pulse of the *Tiberis'* summer flow

To bob along like bloated meat

a nobody nudging the bank.

OBSESSION

By the time we reach the shrine
                                        to *Venus Cloacina*
Cicero's intractable, insisting
                                        this and that

                                        for my own good

Then he rails on about Clodia again:

'It was she who began this trend
Of ming-ling with the city's
                                        lower
                                                        elements …
                                That's right!
                        She takes her friends to the *tabernae,*
With whoops of elation, as the din of music gets higher, they
                        dance!
                                Yes dance,
                                        the ultimate mark of reprobates!
No doubt about it,
                                she's leading her society friends into the mire …'

He leans forward and mutters,

'And what's worse! These Plebeian nights are becoming the latest hit!

                                        But that's not the extent of it …
                                You know that private pleasure park of hers?
Near the *Tiberis* … that stretch of land on the *Campus Martius?*
Well! She's holding banquets there   for a very *in* set.
Snails in milk, pickled octopus; she e-ven manages to get
                                        oy-sters trawled from Bai-a-e …

She …   swans around with her …   blush   of boys,

in tents on the grassy bank …
… hers notable for its stripes of red and white -
That's right,'
Cicero mutters,
'these hypersophisticates don't give a rat's tail
about being discrete.

Clodia even rolls up the tent flaps to let in the view …'

Of the *Tiberis*?
'No, no, no!'
Cicero's strident tone

'The place o-verlooks where the young boys swim …
opp-osite the *Trigarium* …

Their bodies … sprouting into manhood … their taut thighs
and muscled shoulders … glazed with olive oil … dazzling in the sun'

He sighs as if it pains him

'Cicero, you can't be serious!'

He registers my incredulous look
and cricks his neck emphatically.

Then he stubbornly juts out his double chin
as if to free each word
wedged in his throat

'Their *togae praetextae* and *bullae*
left … on the bank …
afford them no

pro…tec…tion …'

50 – 42BCE

AMOR SERVAE (DELICATI'S SATURNALIA)

I've learnt her tastes   to serve her well:

Now I share her tastes: Nothing less than honey.

So let today recline with certain

sticky

Leave me   *infames,*

glazed looks

after many viscous

hours.

Let syrup-lipped Alexandrines   caress my

hands, file my nails, keep them trim.

Let luscious-looking spice-mistress glide like   apéritif,

Serve me wine in a small silver cup; let her service seek my brim.

Serve *mulsum*, spiced for the season. Give me reason to

savour the bouquet, linger lips upon the rim:

Let today's surreptitious tongue slip in,

seeking honey.

Let today serve me a delicacy:

Roasted dormice, *glires,* glazed with honey,

rolled in poppy seeds that spill:

Today let someone else eat

After I've had my fill.

Let me feed the musicians today.

By hand: their own must be free to stray,

unfettered but for strings.

Globi melliti: These honeyed cheese fritters whet appetites.

Soon they'll sing melismatic notes for me. Soon we'll play.

We may get so sticky we'll need to wash today.

I've learnt her tastes

To serve her well:

Now I share her tastes.

Mount Hymettus honey: the bees' knees

Hover over fields of wild thyme.

CORNELIA, ON THE DEATH OF POMPEY

From the deck of the *trireme*
I see my Pompey rise to his feet
Within earshot his question, and then his retort,
'Achillas?
Septimius?
Salvias?

Why no answer from my silent companions?'

Blades are drawn.
Blows rain down.

You raise your toga over your face with both hands
and moan, long and low.

The keel of the boat groans against the sand
Where boy King Ptolemy X111
in purple robes and diadem stands
assembled with his people.
To greet you, ostensibly. To greet you.

Lapped by small ripples of water
Your body's flotsam on the shore
Your toga animated with a reddening swirl

I fold your son into my gown

Determined he won't see
his father's head
walk away with a different man

COIN

Caesar studies both sides of the *denarius* in his hand
then looks at me,

'It's time for a change, Calpurnia!
I've had it with the heads of Saturn and Flora,
                    the busts of Uenus and Diana,
... Hercules with his crown and lion-skin
                                        What about an
                                    eagle ...
                    with a cuirass and shield?'

Caesar's not asking me:
Yet while he paces the length of the *atrium* —
the denarius still turning
                                    over and over
                                            in his contemplative fingers —

I envision his next coin

a coin   as never before   bearing a man
    a man of might   but not a god

His profile   head and bust   facing right

CICERO'S LETTER TO TIRO

You've recently asked about Caesar.
I've news, most shocking,
He's dead.
Apparently a soothsayer warned,
'Beware the Ides of March'

But Caesar … Caesar who refused a bodyguard …
drew attention to his health …

'But the Ides are not passed yet '
Observed the soothsayer …
for it was only the 10th hour of day …

As you know, about a year ago
Caesar declared himself *Imperator in perpetuo*
And adopted the dress of Rome's past kings

One or two fell for it:

Tiro, do you recall, I told you how one Senator proposed
Caesar should be allowed any woman he
please, for the purpose of creating children;
Mind you, with Caesar's reputation, we
Senators imagined this ruling would effect
Nothing other than the status quo!

But I digress … and so Tiro,
It seems the gods have chosen:

Caesar lies, cold, at the stone cold feet of Pompey.

Everything's on sale at his place.
His mark's erased.

SPECULATION

'You say Mark Antony won't be successor?
Just you wait: he'll grow like a new limb to the tree.'

Atticus spreads his hands over the crackling brazier:
The burning bristles making the crisp air smell porcine

'You know, Cicero, he alleges descent from Hercules…'

'Look', I cut in,
'There's only his bullish features to prove it:
His two-name in-heri-tance has been fed
to the swine.'

My finger stabs the complicit air
As I would the chest of an unspeaking culprit

'Mark my words, he's plebeian
… hardy as a roadside weed.'

'*Antony*, in charge of Rome?'
Atticus slaps his knee

'His outraged debtors chased his tail
from Asia to Gaul!
He's a profligate husband
bride-Rome can't afford!'

'Alright then, Atticus,' I blurt out opportunistically,
'Give me your word.
You'll cast your vote for me
When I campaign
against Antony.'

EULOGY (CLODIA'S POEM FOR DELICATI)

This poem this altar this ash is the tomb of Delicati, once a slave:

Here, this dust, let's say it was a hand

I held that hand

Had I been a ring on that hand …

Imagine …

The freedom

To accompany publicly

My private beloved

Be the ring she never removes

Despite envious eyes

Following her bountiful gesture.

LETTER FROM CICERO, or PHILIPPIC 2.6

Atticus, I am sending you a speech,
The second *Philippic*
To be kept back and put out at your discretion

You may find it a violent denunciation of Antony

CICERO'S LETTER TO TIRO, or FEARFUL

My last letter has never arrived?
That bearer is such a rascal ...

Then I must fear for my life
For I can only assume Tiro,
That it has fallen into the wrong hands

Hands that will lift my head for the blade

Mine are not the sort of letters
Which can miss their destination
                                        no harm done

And why should I not be safe at Rome?

But that is not the question

and I am not overmuch concerned about it

What I *am* concerned about you see

So I am coming home.

PROSCRIPTIO

The word on the street is:
Time to settle scores.

Top of the hit list:
                    Cicero
Whose trenchant insults
Have earned him the hatchet

Then Brutus and Cassius

And the Eastern leaders
Who supported them

Name upon name

Two thousand in all.

CICERO'S LETTER TO TIRO, or BOUNTY

I don't know what to do
And after all, the talk may be more
                                                            than the thing.
The thing. The thing.

At this point in time
I cannot call it by its name.

I need not tell you, Tiro, for you already know.
I have it on good word: Antony's men, coming after me.
For what? For the *Philippics*: He makes no bones about it.

You ask what I will do
Either I flee by sea before the ports are closed to me
Or I lay low.

With only lukewarm support perhaps it's better that I go

But if
               the thing is
                              unavoidable;
                                                            Tiro, what then?

NAILED ON THE ROSTRA

'They've left Cicero's eyes   open …'

Calpurnia blows in like the *etesiae,*
                    the dog days' north winds,

non-stop talk
                    echoing in the *tablinum*

'When the young assemble
they'll
no
longer
drink in his oratory   like mother's milk.'

I'm readying to go to *Baiae*
and unfortunately for Calpurnia, it's yesterday's news

Cicero's severed head
          severed hands

For the words he penned.
For the names he named.

EPILOGUE

ARTIFICE

Were you so bruised by the force of my thighs
That now you conceal your public blush?

Why, look to your darkened doorways:
There your fellow Romans gather
To be shucked like oysters;
From there, your fellow Romans scuttle home,
Avoiding public lather, as shadows drink
The pink and orange dawn.

If I've pulled back your hood
It was only to reveal your unkempt decadence,
Your sordid disorder.

I've no disguises.
A woman in my position cannot remain unknown;
Strangers hold no title:

But because you set eyes on me
And called me names
You're compelled to think of me:

Rich, beautiful and imperishable
I rise before you.

LAST WORDS

Stranger, my message is short.
Stop and read it.
This is the unlovely tomb of a lovely woman.
Her parents gave her the name Claudia.
She loved her husband with all her heart.
She bore two children,
one of whom she left on earth,
the other beneath it.
She had a pleasing way of talking and walking.
She tended the house and worked wool.
I have said my piece. Go your way.

AFTER WORD

No. I'll write my own epitaph, leaving
flesh on the bones.
Perhaps one day they'll find it.
Airless, tight-arse wedged in old ceramic,
an original codex in a poor state;
frequent *lacunae* attributable
to the random gnawing of a rat.

NOTES

Nothing Sacred is a work of fiction that draws its stimulus and direction from historical sources about late Republican Rome, and which developed from a fascination with the etymologies of Latin and Greek, and the longevity of sexual metaphor since antiquity. Following are notes that are not in any way essential to the understanding or enjoyment of *Nothing Sacred,* but I hope some readers will find them interesting or useful.

admissarius - stallion (L.)

alipilus - slave employed to pluck body hair (L.)

alium - garlic (Gk.)

Allobroge (s) - person from that region (L.)

amphora (ae) – receptacle with two handles and a narrow neck (L.)

'And why should I not be safe at Rome? But that is not the question and I am not overmuch concerned about it What I *am* concerned about you see So I am coming home' - cf *Cicero* "And why should I not be as safe in rome as Marcellus? But that is not the question and I am not overmuch concerned about it. What I *am* concerned about you see. So I am coming home." In *Letters to Atticus* Volume IV Letter 426 (XVI.15). D.R Shackleton Bailey (Ed. & Trans.,) Cambridge., MA & London: Harvard University Press 1999

atrium, atrio - courtyard in the centre of a private home with a large opening in the ceiling to admit light (L.)

auguraculum - a space in and from which the augurs interpreted natural signs as an indication of divine approval or disapproval of a proposed event or action (L.)

Bithynia - An ancient region, kingdom and Roman province in the north-west of Asia Minor

Baiae - With its temperate climate, attractive location on the shores of the Bay of Naples, and natural springs, Baiae was a desirable resort area where the Republican elite built their luxurious villas

beccafia - fig-peckers (L.)

Bona Dea - annual festival of the 'good goddess' (L.)

bulbi - edible bulb, (L.) here intended to imply its use as an aphrodisiac

bullae - A *bulla* was a golden ornament, an amulet (of Etruscan origin) worn by boys of good family. They laid it aside on receiving the *toga virilis* (L.)

cacat!- 'shit!' expletive (L.)

canis (canem) - dogs (L.)

caput - head (L.)

cephi - apes (L.)

cervi - deer (L.)

chiroptera - bat (L.)

CICERO: LETTER TO ATTICUS - cf Cicero's account in Letter 75 (IV.3) in *Cicero: Letters to Atticus* Volume I. D.R Shackleton Bailey (Ed. & Trans.,) Cambridge., MA & London: Harvard University Press 1999

cinaedus – kinaedos (Gk.) According to Skinner, a kinaedos was a kind of dancer whose movements, accompanied by the rattle of a tambourine, included wriggling of the buttocks. Skinner, Marilyn B. *Sexuality in Greek and Roman Culture*. Oxford, Malden, Carlton: Blackwell Publishing, 2005.

Circus Maximus - an open air track used for horse drawn chariot-racing, gladiator contests and ludi. In 46BC a moat was constructed between the arena and the wooden seating tiers; this surrounded the track except at the *carcares* end, where the chariot stalls were located. Around the outside of the building was a single storey arcade containing shops.

Cloaca Maxima – sewer draining from the Forum to the Tiber (L.)

CLODIUS' GANG – cf Petrarch *Life of Pompey;* Tom Holland *Rubicon,* 2003, p. 251

cognomen – surname, a Roman's third name, usually hereditary, differentiating families within the same *gens.* Other *cognomina* were honorific, sometimes taken from a conquered country. Women generally had only one clan name which they retained after marriage (L.)

cohabitus - *cohabito* (L.) to dwell together

Colchis - the eastern Black Sea region in antiquity

comitiorum, comitia - an assembly of all roman citizens (L.)

consul - highest of the roman magistrates; two were elected, usually in July, to take office on the following 1 January; minimal age of forty-three (L.)

contio - public open-air meeting held by either Consuls or Tribunes ; function of the state, governed by specific rules. (L.)

convivium, convivial - Rooms for entertainment – citizen Romans of both sexes reclined and dined together, and female members of a household could mix with external men. Traditionally there were nine places in a three couch Roman banquet, three to a couch hence these formal dining rooms were called *triclinia.* Slaves were continually needed to pass around food and wine since reclining diners had no individual plates and were not able to reach the central table (L.)

cubicula, cubiculum - Not modern concept of bedroom. These were relatively small rooms, often no more than two metres wide, suitable as private spaces for individuals. Their positions often left them more exposed to public inspection especially when they immediately adjoined and interconnected with Triclinia. They were regularly used in the day for private meetings, for the reception of intimate friends, or the conducting of confidential business (L.)

cubile - Sleeping couch (L.)

culina - food preparation room (L.)

culli, cunni - arseholes, cunts (L.)

culus - metaphorical for buttocks (Gk.)

curia (ae) - meeting house(s) of the Senate (L.) The original senate house of Rome, situated on the north side of the comitium, the Curia Hostilia, was burnt down in the riots after Clodius' death, and later rebuilt. In 44BC, Caesar initiated the building of a new Senate house, Curia Iulia.

Deliciae - According to Fitzgerald, this is a complex word, denoting at the same time objects or beings, a status (favourite, darling) and a form of behaviour; to call something or somebody your *delicati* is to point in two opposite directions, to the object and to oneself, and it is also to mark one's behaviour, quite self-consciously, as questionable (L.) Fitzgerald, William. *Catullan Provocations: Lyric Poetry and the Drama of Position.* Classics and Contemporary Thought. Ed. Tom Habinek. Los Angeles & London: University of California Press, 1995.

denarius (*denarii*) - silver coin most generally in use, equal to four sesterces (L.)

eheu - Oh no! (L.)

emporium - dockyards, marketplace, trading centre (L.)

Esquiline - *Esquiliae*; an area of high ground east of the city with two raised projections, Mons Oppius and Mons Cispius; later known as Mons Esquilinus.

etesiae - northerly winds which blew every year during the Dog days (L.)

exedra - a large curving space set back from a colonnade (L. from Gk.)

exoleti - 'over-aged' male prostitutes (L.) Skinner, Marilyn B. *Sexuality in Greek and Roman Culture.* Oxford, Malden, Carlton: Blackwell Publishing, 2005.

fascinum - apotraic charm; amulets in the shape of a phallus, worn around the neck, for the purpose of warding off the evil eye.(L.)

'fern, forest, nest' - filix, pilus, pecten (L.) = pubic hair

flammeum - the colour was thought to represent the bride's bloodshed at her first sexual encounter. (L.)

flokati - shag pile sheep's wool rug (Gk.)

fontes - fountain (L.)

fortitudo - strength; moral bravery; courage, valour (L.)

Forum - market place; centre of political activity (L.)

fut'uo - fuck, as expletive (pron. *foot-oo-oh)* (L.)

galabeyas - men's traditional long loose-fitting garment with full sleeves (Ar.)

garum - sauce made from the salted entrails of fish (L.)

glires - edible dormice (L.)

haemorrhagia - haemorrhage (L.)

haruspices - soothsayers, diviners, inspectors of entrails (L.)

'He hasn't got a bow for his arrows / says the mistress of the house,/he hasn't even got a sling' - In *The Latin Sexual Vocabulary*, Adams J.N. (1982) discusses the use of weapons as sexual metaphors, including the bow, and the sling = *mentula* (penis) + *petrae* (testicles) London: Duckworth & Co Ltd, 1982.

'high birth beauty wealth health wit , and conspicuous intelligence' - cf Thornton Wilder p. 11 "there is a Great Giver who gave Clodia beauty, health, wealth, high birth, and conspicuous intelligence" in *The Ides of March*. London; New York; Longmans, Green and Co., 1948

humours - In Hippocratic theory, these bodily substances, if imbalanced, could affect personality and physical health (Gk.)

Ides of March - In the roman calendar, the 15th day in March, May, July, and October; or the 13th in the other months.

'I expect you have heard, Tiro' - cf Cicero, "'I imagine you will have heard" Cicero's account of the Bona Dea. Letters 12 (I.12) and 13 (I.13) in *Cicero: Letters to Atticus* Volume I. D.R Shackleton Bailey (Ed. & Trans.,) Cambridge., MA & London: Harvard University Press 1999

'I'll trump the 'blurts' of Catullus' gossiping door' - Catullus' Poem 67 consists of a dialogue between Catullus and the door of an unknown woman.

impluvio - a basin in the atrium floor for receiving rain-water from the roof (L.)

Imperator in perpetuo - ruler in perpetuity (L.)

improbe (i) - a dishonest or disreputable person; rascals (Cic.) (L.)

'I'm told gangs are in formation … Even the honest men are yielding to his pleas' - cf Cicero, "Gangs of rough are in formation" and "The honest men are yielding to Clodius' pleas", in Letter 13 (I.13) in *Cicero: Letters to Atticus*

Volume I. D.R Shackleton Bailey (Ed. & Trans.,) Cambridge., MA & London: Harvard University Press,1999

infames - lacking reputation, *famis* (L.)

insanus - mad, raging, insane, demented (L.)

'I personally …' - cf Thornton Wilder p. 16 "I personally don't believe that she poisoned her husband or that she has had improper relations with her brothers, but thousands do believe it" in *The Ides of March*. London; New York; Longmans, Green and Co., 1948

'It's not just the speech-making at every meeting, he uses my name to stir up ill feeling' - cf Cicero, "When Clodius had betoken himself to speech-making at meetings and used my name to stir up ill feeling,", in Letter 16 (I.16) in *Cicero: Letters to Atticus* Volume I. D.R Shackleton Bailey (Ed. & Trans.,) Cambridge., MA & London: Harvard University Press 1999

Janus - God of endings and beginnings (L.)

kolós kai vrakí - idiomatic expression; as close as buttocks and underwear (Gk.)

kouroi - male youths represented in Greek sculpture dating from the Archaic Period (Gk.)

lacunae - cavities, gaps (L.) here intended to mean holes.

LAST WORDS - With the exception of its title, this poem quotes *Corpus of Latin Inscriptions,* CIL 6. 15346.

leporium - enclosure for keeping hares (L.)

litter - a curtained vehicular couch atop two parallel poles, carried by slaves (L.)

matronas -roman freewomen; matrons (L.)

'may my writing burn girls, burn boys' - after Propertius 3.2.10

meretrix, meretrices - female prostitute (s) (L.)

'Mine are not the sort of letters that can miss their destination no harm done' - cf Cicero, "Mine are not the sort of letters which can miss their destination and no harm done." In Letter 91 (VI.17) in *Cicero: Letters to Atticus* Volume I. D.R Shackleton Bailey (Ed. & Trans.,) Cambridge., MA & London: Harvard University Press 1999

mirabile - wonderful, marvellous, astonishing, extraordinary (L.)

modius, modii - a dry measure (L.)

mulsum - spiced honeyed wine (L.)

munera - lit. 'rewards', ***munera*** were spectacles such as gladiatorial combats, wild animal shows, and other unusual exhibitions (L.)

nobiles - man of noble birth (L.)

nomen - a Roman's hereditary gens or clan name, usually ending in –ius (L.)

nones - the fifth day of each month (L.)

olisbos - dildo (L.)

o po' po' - utterance of exasperation (Gk.)

opus - sexual metaphor of 'work', spec. to male part in intercourse (L.)

ordo propria - (L.) here intended as 'the done thing'

pallium - a woolen cloak (L.)

papyrum - papyrus, a material similar to paper, from the papyrus plant, Cyperus papyrus, native to the Nile river valley

parazonium - long dagger (L.)

pardi - leopard (L.)

Pater Patriae - protector of the Republic (L.)

patricians (patricios) - male citizens of the senatorial class (L.)

peplos - a women's sleeveless dress made from two rectangular pieces of cloth partially sewn together on both sides. Two large pins connected at the shoulderline and the waistline was belted or tied (L.)

peristylium - colonnaded garden (L.)

Philippics - Cicero wrote fourteen speeches, almost all of which were attacks on Antony, and to which he gave the title of 'Philippics'. *Marcus Tullius Cicero: Ten Speeches,* James E.G. Zetgel (Intro. & Trans.,), Hackett Publishing Company, Inc. Indianapolis.

pisces - fish (L.)

poetria - poetess (L.), here implied to be an amateur poet; a poetaster

popina(e) - food house (L.)

populares - Men of politics, in general men of the senatorial class who wished their deeds and words to be pleasing to the multitude (L.)

praenomen - given name (L.)

praetor - second in rank of the annual magistrates who held administrative roles and spent a year in office (L.)

PROSCRIPTIO - Proscription (L.). The publication of a list of persons who were declared outlaws and whose property was confiscated. This method was used by Antony, Lepidus and Octavian, the triumvirs of 43 BC, to rid themselves of their political and personal enemies.

puticuli - mass burial pits for paupers and slaves according to ancient sources

'quiff and smirk' - Pompey, by association with the cow-lick of hair on his forehead, and his grin

rostra - the speaker's platform, so named from the beaks (rostra) of captured ships which decorated it (L.)

Sacra Via - The Sacred Way; the oldest and most famous street in Rome. It was also a residential quarter in republican times

saleb - the root of a type of orchid, considered to be an aphrodisiac (L.)

Saturnalia - Inversion of the social order, celebrated in the mid-winter festival of Saturn. People gave each other presents, the shops closed, and an air of licence and merry-making prevailed.

scaena - Latin term derived from ancient greek; stage (L.)

'scratch this lesson in wax' - wooden tablets coated with wax and fastened together with thread were used for memoranda and short notes

sentinella - sentinel (Ital.)

Servian Wall - *Murus Servii Tullii* (L.) some sections of the city wall of ancient Rome are ascribed to King Servius Tullius of the sixth century BC; other sections to the fourth century

servitium amoris; amor servae - The slavery of love; the love of a slave (L.)

sesquiculus - arsehole and a half (L.)

sestertius (sesterces) - bronze coin worth about a quarter of a denarius (L.)

'she's being served a specialty dinner' - The sexual position of a woman astride a man was considered unusual

spelt - An ancient grain, a relative of wheat with a nutty flavour

'step longer than my leg' - Idiom (Ital.) 'non fare il passo piu lungo della gamba'

'So you see, Tiro, he's taken to giving me a public bloodletting, in drips and drops. It's not just the speech-making at every meeting, he uses my name to stir up ill-feeling' - cf Cicero, "Clodius had betaken himself to speech-making at meetings and used my name to stir up ill-feeling, ye gods, what battles, what havoc I made!" In Letter 16 (I.16) in *Cicero: Letters to Atticus* Volume 1. D.R Shackleton Bailey (Ed. & Trans.,) Cambridge., MA & London: Harvard University Press 1999

sotto voce - In an undertone (Ital.)

spicarae - white bait (L.)

stola - a long outer garment worn by Roman matrons (L.)

strigil (es) - a hollow curved instrument used to cleanse oil and dirt from perspired bodies (L.)

struthiocameli - ostriches (L.)

sub rosa - under the roses (L.)

Suburae - a quarter of Rome, north east of the Forum

suffragatores - voters, supporters (L.)

'Suns can westward ... ' - cf Catullus' poem *To Lesbia*

symposium - drinking parties (Gk.), but here intended to mean poetic contests organised by the elite

taberna vetera (e)(us) - old Shop (s) (L.)

tabella suffragium - voting tablet (L.)

tablinum - the large reception room of a Roman *domus* (L.)

'Take in the pin' - According to Edwards, gladiators were sometimes infibulated – that is, a pin was inserted through their foreskins – to prevent them from having sex, and to preserve their energies for public performance. Edwards, Catharine. *The Politics of Immorality in Ancient Rome.* Cambridge: Cambridge University Press, 1993.

testis - personification of the penis. (L.) *The Latin Sexual Vocabulary*, Adams J.N. (1982) London: Duckworth & Co Ltd, 1982.

Temple of Jupiter Stator - a temple of ancient Rome where the Senate met to hear Cicero's oration against Cataline in 63

The twelve tables - The earliest code of Roman law dating circa 452BC

'the edging to my teeth, a metallic bluish black' - a symptom of lead poisoning

tragi - a type of fish (L.)

tragoedia - tragedy (L.)

Trigarium - a place where horses were exercised (L.)

trireme - maritime warship with three oars to a bench (Gk.)

triumvirs - the three leaders in power in a triumvirate (L.)

Tulliano - Tullianum; a prison (carcer) in the Forum Romanum (L.)

ursi - bears (L.)

vanitas - vanity (L)

veni, vidi, vici - Trans. *I came, I saw, I conquered.* Delivered by Julius Caesar to the Roman Senate describing his victory over Pharnaces II of Pontus in the Battle of Zela

verba nuptae - Obscenities of the bedroom uttered by women. Adams J.N. *The Latin Sexual Vocabulary* London: Duckworth & Co Ltd, 1982.

veritas - truth (L.)

vestibulum - long narrow hallway leading from the front door to the *atrium* in a roman house (L.)

Via Appia - principal route to Southern Italy, leading from Rome to Capua (later to Brundisium), built in 312 BC

vici (vicos) - high street (s)

Vicus Tuscus - The shortest connection between the Roman Forum and the Circus Maximus, also known as "Etruscan Alley"

vino - wine (L.)

vir - male citizen (L.)

WOULD BE SACRED - cf Thornton Wilder pp. 2-3 "What's to be done? I have inherited this burden of superstition and nonsense. I govern innumerable men but must acknowledge that I am governed by birds and thunderclaps. All this frequently obstructs the operation of the State; it closes the doors of the Senate and the Courts for days and weeks at a time … but what can I do against the apathy that tells me that Rome will be saved by overwatching Gods or is resigned to the fact that Rome will come to ruin because the Gods are maleficent? I am not given to brooding, but often I find myself brooding over this matter." In *The Ides of March.* London; New York; Longmans, Green and Co., 1948

BIBLIOGRAPHY

Adams, James N. *The Latin Sexual Vocabulary*. London: Duckworth & Co Ltd, 1982.

Aldrete, Gregory S. *Daily Life in the Roman City: Rome, Pompeii, and Ostia*. Westport CT: Greenwood Press, 2004.

Beerden, Kim. 'A conspicuous Meal: Fattening Dormice, Snails and Thrushes in the Roman World.' *Petit Propos Culinaires* 90 (2010): 79-98.

Cantarella, Eva. *The Role and Status of Women in Greek and Roman Antiquity*. Trans. Maureen B. Fant. Baltimore and London: The John Hopkins University Press, 1981.

Catullus. *The Complete Poems of Catullus*. Trans. David Mulroy. London and Wisconsin: University of Wisconsin Press, 2002.

Catullus. *Catullus the Poems*. Trans. Peter Whigham. London and New York: Penguin, 2004.

Cicero, Marcus Tullius. *Selected Political Speeches of Cicero*. Trans. Michael Grant. Baltimore: Penguin Books, 1969.

Cicero, Marcus Tullius. *Letters to Atticus*. Volumes I-IV. Edited and trans. D.R. Shackleton Bailey. Cambridge MA and London: Harvard University Press, 1999.

Cicero, Marcus Tullius. *Marcus Tullius Cicero: Ten Speeches*. Introduction and trans. James E.G. Zetzel.

Indianapolis: Hackett Publishing Company, Inc, 2009.

Corbeill, Anthony. *Controlling Laughter: Political Humor in the Late Roman Republic.* Princeton: Princeton University Press, 1996.

Corpus of Latin Inscriptions, Berlin: Berlin-Brandenburg Academy of Sciences and Humanities, 2010. http://cil.bbaw.de/cil_en/index_en.html.

Cross, Suzanne. *Feminae Romanae:The Women of Ancient Rome.* 2001-2004. http://dominae.fwsl.com/Influence/Clodia/Index.html.

Dalby, Andrew. 'The Satyrica Concluded.' *Gastronomica* Fall, 2005.

Dillon, Matthew; Garland, Linda., eds. *Ancient Rome: From the Early Republic to the Assassination of Julius Caesar.* London and New York: Routledge, 2005.

Diotima: Materials for the Study of Women and Gender in the Ancient World., Ed. Ross Scaife. 2011. http://www.stoa.org/diotima/

Dominik, William J., ed. *Roman Eloquence: Rhetoric in Society and Literature.* London and New York: Routledge, 1997.

Dorey, T.A., ed. *Cicero.* London: Routledge & Kegan Paul, 1964.

Edwards, Catharine. *The Politics of Immorality in Ancient Rome.* Cambridge: Cambridge University Press, 1993.

Edwards, Catharine. *Writing Rome. Textual Approaches to the City.* Cambridge: Cambridge University Press, 1996.

Fitzgerald, William. *Catullan Provocations: Lyric Poetry and the Drama of Position.* Classics and Contemporary Thought., ed. Tom Habinek. Los Angeles and London: University of California Press, 1995.

Fitzgerald, William. *Slavery and the Roman Literary Imagination.* Roman Literature and its Contexts. Cam-

bridge: Cambridge University Press, 2000.
Frank, Tenney. *Catullus and Horace. Two Poets in Their Environment.* New York: Russell & Russell, 1965.
Gardner, Jane F. *Women in Roman Law and Society.* London and Sydney: Croom Helm, 1986.
Hallett, Judith P; Skinner, Marilyn B., eds. *Roman Sexualities.* Princeton: Princeton University Press, 1997.
Henderson, Jeffrey, ed. *The Digital Loeb Classical Library.* Cambridge MA: Harvard University Press, 2015. http://www.loebclassics.com.
Holland, Tom. *Rubicon: The Triumph and Tragedy of the Roman Republic.* London: Abacus, 2004.
Hurley, Amanda Kolson. *Catullus.* Ancients in Action. London: Bristol Classical Press, 2004.
James, Sharon L. *Learned Girls and Male Persuasion: Gender and Reading in Roman Love Elegy.* Berkeley; Los Angeles; London: University of California Press, 2003.
Keith, A.M. *Engendering Rome. Women in Latin Epic.* Roman Literature and Its Contexts. Eds. Denis Feeney & Stephen Hinds. Cambridge: Cambridge University Press, 2000.
Kleiner, Diana.E.E., and Matheson, Susan B. *I Claudia: Women in Ancient Rome.* New Haven: Yale University Art Gallery, 1996.
Kyle, Donald. G. *Spectacles of Death in Ancient Rome.* London and New York: Routledge, 1998.
Matyszak, Philip. *Chronicle of the Roman Republic. The Rulers of Ancient Rome from Romulus to Augustus.* London: Thames & Hudson, 2003.
McManus, Barbara; Bonefas, Suzanne. *V-Roma: A Virtual Community for Teaching and Learning Classics.* The College of New Rochelle, 2003. http://vroma.org/
Parker, Holt N. 'The Teratogenic Grid.' *Roman Sexualities.* Eds. Judith P Skinner & Marilyn B. Hallett.

Princeton, New Jersey: Princeton University Press, 1977.

Perseus Digital Library. Ed. Gregory R. Crane. Massachusetts: Tufts University, 1985. http://www.perseus.tufts.edu.

Platner, Samuel Ball. *A Topographical Dictionary of Ancient Rome.* Completed and rev. Thomas Ashby. London: Humphrey Milford. Oxford University Press, 1929.

Plutarch. *Plutarch's Lives –Pompey.* Loeb Classical Library. Cambridge MA: Harvard University Press, 2015. DOI: 10.4159/DLCL.plutarch-lives_pompey.1917.

Pomeroy, Sarah B. *Goddesses, Whores, Wives and Slaves. Women in Classical Antiquity.* Second ed. New York: Schocken Books, 1995.

Porter, J. *C. Valerius Catullus.* Saskatoon, SK, Canada: University of Saskatchewan, 2003. www.duke.usak.ca/~porterj/CourseNotes/CatullusNotes.html.

Raia, Ann R., and Sebesta, Judith Lynn. *Online Companion to The Worlds of Roman Women.* Updated 2015. http://www2.cnr.edu/home/sas/araia/companion.html.

Raia, Ann., Luschnig, Cecelia., and Sebesta, Judith Lynn. *The Worlds of Roman Women.* Indianapolis: Hackett Publishing, 2005.

Richardson, N.J. *The Homeric Hymn to Demeter.* Oxford: Oxford University Press, 1974.

Scaife, Ross and Bonefas, Suzanne. *Diotima: Materials for the Study of Women and Gender in the Ancient World.* 1995. www.stoa.org/diotima/html.

Skinner, Marilyn B. *Sexuality in Greek and Roman Culture.* Oxford, Malden, Carlton: Blackwell Publishing, 2005.

Sallust. *The Jugurthine War / The Conspiracy of Catiline.*

Trans and Introduction. S.A. Handford. London: Penguin Books, 1963.

Treggiari, Susan. *Terentia, Tullia and Publilia. The Women of Cicero's Family*. London and New York: Routledge, 2007.

Watson, A. *Roman Slave Law*. Baltimore: John Hopkins University Press, 1987.

Wilder, Thornton. *The Ides of March*. London; New York; Toronto: Longmans, Green and Co., 1948.

Wray, David. *Catullus and the Poetics of Roman Manhood*. Cambridge, Massachussetts: Cambridge University Press, 2001.

ACKNOWLEDGEMENTS

Poems from *Nothing Sacred* have previously appeared in *Rabbit, Bukker Tillibul,* in *Long Glances: A snapshot of new Australian poetry from the inaugural Jean Cecily Drake-Brockman Prize, Mascara Literary Journal* and in *Muse.* Excerpts were also presented at two conferences: Truth or Beauty: Poetry and Biography, Victoria University, Wellington New Zealand, 26-28 November 2014 and Straddling the Divide: Reception Studies Today, The University of Melbourne, 1-2 December, 2011.

I gratefully acknowledge the people and support that helped me, in one way or another, complete this verse novel: an APA scholarship at The University of Melbourne; Kevin Brophy for his guidance and thoughtful reading of early drafts; Heather Jackson, Honorary Research Fellow at The University of Melbourne, School of Historical Studies, Centre for Classics and Archaeology, for her assistance with latin conjugation; and my partner and friends for their patience and encouragement.

BIOGRAPHICAL NOTE

Poems by Linda Weste have been published in *Best Australian Poetry* and Australian literary journals. She lives in Melbourne. *Nothing Sacred* is her first novel.

Printed in Australia
Ingram Content Group Australia Pty Ltd
AUHW021235021123
385929AU00002B/17

9 781925 333220